THE BOY WHO STEPPED THROUGH TIME

ANNA CIDDOR

ALLEN&UNWIN

SYDNEY • MELBOURNE • AUCKLAND • LONDON

First published by Allen & Unwin in 2021

Allen & Unwin
83 Alexander Street
Crows Nest NSW 2065
Australia
Phone: (61 2) 8425 0100
Email: info@allenandunwin.com
Web: www.allenandunwin.com

A catalogue record for this book is available from the National Library of Australia

ISBN 978 1 76052 644 3

For teaching resources, explore
www.allenandunwin.com/resources/for-teachers

Cover illustration by Kate Moon
Internal illustrations by Anna Ciddor
Set in 12.25/16pt Bembo by Midlands Typesetters, Australia
Printed in Australia in March 2021 by McPherson's Printing Group

www.annaciddor.com

10 9 8 7 6 5 4 3 2 1

THE BOY WHO STEPPED THROUGH TIME

Also by Anna Ciddor

52 Mondays
The Family with Two Front Doors
Runestone
Wolfspell
Stormriders
Night of the Fifth Moon

CONTENTS

Villa Rubia

This book would not have been possible without the collaboration of my amazing sister, Tamara Lewit. She inspired me, helped me brainstorm plot ideas, critiqued every word as I wrote it, and used her brilliant skills as a historian and archaeologist to unearth the tiniest details I needed about ancient Romans.

Arelate

1
CAMILLA . . . WHO?

'I CAN'T WEAR THAT!' wailed Perry, when his mother pulled his costume out of the suitcase.

'It's what Roman boys used to wear,' she insisted, dropping it over his head.

'But . . .'

Perry looked in the mirror and groaned. He was wearing a bright yellow dress that reached down to his knees, with big red circles on the skirt and sleeves.

'Why couldn't I just be a soldier?' he grumbled.

'Because we're going to a Roman grape harvest festival, not a battle re-enactment,' said Mum. 'I couldn't let you dress up as a legionary.'

Perry rolled his eyes.

'I copied a picture of a boy from late Roman times,' Mum went on. 'It's . . .'

'Authentic!' yelled Perry and his big sister together, and they both started laughing. 'Authentic' was Mum's favourite word because she couldn't just say 'correct' like a normal person.

'Well, it *is* authentic,' protested Mum. 'I even made it for you in my weaving class.'

That explains the lumpy, scratchy wool, thought Perry.

'Actually, I think you look quite cool,' said Melissa, snapping photos of him with her phone.

Mum turned to her suitcase again. 'Melissa and I are getting dressed now. You wait in the guest lounge,' she said.

Perry goggled at her. 'I'm not . . .'

'You can take off the tunic for now,' said Mum, dragging out something blue. 'Just put it on when we get there.'

With a surge of relief, Perry scrambled into shorts and a T-shirt, and kicked his costume under the bed. If he was lucky, they'd forget it and leave it behind.

In the hotel lounge, Dad was scrolling through the sports news on his iPad.

'Did we win?' demanded Perry.

Dad nodded, and leaned back, smiling, in the squeaky leather chair.

'Yes!' cheered Perry. The only bad part about coming on holidays to the south of France was missing out on going to footy matches back in Australia.

'Aren't you supposed to be putting on a costume?' said Dad.

'I'll chuck it on when we get there,' Perry grunted. 'How come Mum hasn't made *you* dress up?'

'Mum knows I never dress up,' chuckled Dad, and went back to reading his news.

Perry stood beside him, fidgeting with the mini high-bounce ball he kept in his pocket, and gazing at the tempting expanse of hard, tiled floor. He slipped the ball from his pocket, bounced it once, and looked around. No one was watching. Grinning, he bounced it again, harder this time. Whoops . . . the fluoro green ball went skittering across the floor. Perry lunged after it, crashed into the wall, and scooped up the ball.

'This is no place to play rough games,' snapped a voice with a posh English accent.

Perry straightened up guiltily. There was a small man, almost hidden in a high-backed armchair, glaring at him over a pair of spectacles.

'You could have damaged that picture,' scolded the man, gesturing at the wall behind Perry. 'That's a rare fragment of Roman wall painting. Nearly two thousand years old.'

3

Perry turned.

A square of glass covered part of the wall, and behind it was a section of old, cracked plaster with flecks of coloured paint on it. Perry looked at it, trying to see how it made a picture. Those green, faded shapes could be leaves, and that might be a thin, curvy tree trunk, and . . .

'Hey Dad, check this out,' he said, hurrying back to his father. 'There's an old Roman painting over there. But . . .' He lowered his voice to a whisper. 'Watch out for the old grouch in the armchair.'

Dad turned off his iPad, stretched noisily, and strolled across the room.

The man scowled at them, but went back to reading his book.

Perry pointed at the painting on the wall. 'See?' he whispered. 'It looks like a tree with a cat peeking out.'

Dad tilted his head to one side. 'I think you've got a good imagination,' he said. 'All I can see are green and brown blobs.'

The morning was nearly over by the time Mum and Melissa came downstairs. To Perry's disappointment, Mum was carrying his tunic.

'How do we look?' asked Melissa, and they both twirled around to show off their dangly bead earrings and long dresses with wide, colourful stripes down the front.

Dad raised his eyebrows. 'I thought Romans wore those sheet things – what were they called? Togas?'

'Togas! Women didn't wear togas,' scoffed Mum. 'Anyway . . .' She glanced down at her dress. 'This is late Roman style. When togas weren't the fashion anymore.'

Perry caught Melissa's eye. 'It's authentic, Dad,' they chorused together.

Dad smiled. 'Of course it is,' he said. 'Well, we'd better get going if you want to reach the festival before it finishes.'

Mum slid into the driver's seat of the hire car.

'Don't get us lost, Martin,' she warned, turning to Dad. 'Which way first?'

'Uh . . .' As usual, Dad swivelled his phone round trying to work out the satnav directions.

'Oh, Dad,' snorted Melissa. 'Give it to me. Mum, just go straight,' she instructed.

Then she picked up her own phone again.

'Hey, Perry, everyone loves your costume,' she said, holding the screen towards him.

'Melissa, which way?' screeched Mum, as an intersection loomed in front of them.

'Oops, hang on . . . right, no . . . go round that old Roman ruin.'

'Hey, that's Constantine's bathhouse,' said Perry.

'This is the way we came yesterday when we went to the museum.'

'Don't mention that museum,' groaned Melissa. 'I still can't believe you and Mum spent two *hours* looking at dead people.'

'It wasn't dead people. It was ancient stone coffins. From Roman times,' protested Perry.

'Same thing.'

'Well, they were interesting. I found one of a girl who died when she was exactly my age: eleven years, two months and one day old. Her name . . .'

'You and your numbers,' burst in his big sister. 'Anyway, how do you know? You can't read Latin.'

'I can a bit,' he said. 'Mum was teaching me on the plane, but . . .'

'Mum, Mum, turn here!' shrieked Melissa.

Mum swung the wheel, and the next moment they were zooming down the autoroute.

But Perry's thoughts were still back at the museum. He was trying to remember the name of the girl from that coffin. It had started with C . . . Camilla something? And then he forgot about her as he noticed the other cars flying past so fast they were almost a blur.

'Wow, what's the speed limit here?' he asked.

'I don't think there is one!' cried Mum.

'I need something to eat,' said Melissa, tapping

on her phone. 'It's ages since breakfast. I'm checking where there's a good cafe.'

'Can we at least get out of Arles first?' pleaded Dad.

2

THE FESTIVAL

THE WORDS WERE BARELY OUT of Dad's mouth before his head was nodding on his chest.

'He's off!' laughed Perry.

Dad always fell asleep the instant he got in a car.

'If he was navigating we'd end up in Italy!' snorted Melissa.

A while later, she was directing Mum to turn off the autoroute at a town called Aix.

'There'll be somewhere to eat here,' she said, peering out the window as they circled a cobbled square with a fountain dancing in the sunshine, and cafes with colourful outdoor tables.

But by the time Mum found a parking spot, Melissa had decided she didn't actually want to go wandering around town wearing a long, stripy robe and a green and gold hairnet on her head.

So Dad was shaken awake, and he and Perry were sent to find snacks while the others waited in the car.

'Not pizza!' Melissa told Perry firmly. 'Some of us like to eat other things.'

'And don't buy too much,' warned Mum, sliding down her window to call after them. 'There'll be plenty of food at the festival. Authentic Roman food.'

Back in the car, Perry plonked a paper bag of croissants on the seat between himself and his sister, and handed her a drink.

'Phew, it's hot out there,' he said.

'It was about a million degrees waiting in here,' said Melissa. She eyed him taking two croissants from the bag. 'We're about to have a Roman feast, remember.'

Perry glanced at his mother chatting to Dad and sipping her coffee, and leaned towards his sister. 'The Romans ate mice,' he said in a hoarse whisper, 'and some sort of mouldy, stinky fish sauce. It says so in that book Mum gave us.'

Melissa pulled a face and quickly took another croissant for herself. Perry pressed the cool *limonade* against his cheek before he yanked off the lid, managing not to fizz *too* much of the drink all over the car.

Mum turned and smiled at them.

'Uh oh, I recognise that smile,' said Melissa. 'It's tidbit time.'

Mum laughed. She always tried to make their holidays educational by sharing 'tidbits' with them.

'Aix was founded by the Romans,' she announced, 'but the Roman name for Aix was Aquae Sextiae. Aqua was the Latin word for water, and—'

'Whoa,' interrupted Dad, 'I hope we're not looking for Roman ruins here or we'll never get to that festival.'

'No, no,' said Mum quickly.

'Well, let's get going then,' said Dad. 'It must be still an hour to the Taradel Winery.'

'Righty-o,' said Mum, starting the car. 'Off we go for our journey back in time!'

As they zoomed along the autoroute, Perry began to worry about his costume again. 'I bet all the other boys will have soldier costumes,' he muttered to Melissa. 'And I've got to put on that dress!'

But his sister was concentrating on the satnav. 'Mum, turn off the autoroute here,' she called.

A few minutes later they were driving down a country road, with vineyards stretching in all directions.

'What's that?' asked Perry, pointing at something that looked like a broken column standing alone by the side of the road.

'Oh,' cried Mum excitedly, 'it must be a Roman milestone. This is the route of an old Roman road. They had stones with Roman numerals carved on them, to ... *He-e-e-lp!*'

She screeched to a halt. A giant orange contraption had appeared around a bend, trundling down the middle of the road.

'*Zut!*' exclaimed Melissa. She had taken to swearing in French.

They all stared while the monster rolled a few metres, turned in a gate and began to lumber down the rows of grapes, the massive tractor tyres fitting neatly over the vines.

'It's a grape harvester!' said Perry.

As the car sped up again, a roadside sign popped into view. *Château Taradel 100m* it read, and a poster taped beneath it proclaimed:

FESTIVAL
1ᵉʳ SEPTEMBRE
UNE JOURNÉE ROMAINE

'That's it!'

'Dad, wake up, we're nearly there!'

Perry peered from the car windows as they turned down a long gravel driveway. Among the grapevines to his right he spotted a bare patch of earth, almost the size of a footy field, dotted with lines of stones.

'That must be the Roman villa!' cooed Mum.

'I thought a villa was a mansion,' protested Perry.

'You should have been here seventeen hundred years ago,' said Mum, in her explaining voice. 'There would have been a grand, two-storey mansion here with a courtyard in the middle, and barns, pigsties . . .'

'Like your bedroom, Perry,' sniggered Melissa.

'. . . and a bathhouse, pigeon tower, buildings where they made wine and olive oil,' Mum went on. 'And people of course. Dozens of slaves! They looked after the fields and the animals, the master and his family . . .'

The car rounded another vineyard and the château came into sight – an imposing stone staircase leading up to wide double doors, windows with shutters, and water trickling from a lion's head into a stone basin.

With a spatter of gravel, Mum pulled up the car and they threw open their doors.

'We're here!'

Two boys wearing fake Roman helmets ran past, attacking each other with plastic swords.

Perry glared at his mother. 'I told you,' he growled.

'Well, their costumes are all wrong,' said Mum.

There was a wide lawn in front of the château,

with people milling around, and the white shapes of marquees. The air was filled with the smell of cooking and the shrilling of cicadas.

'Quick, Perry, into your costume,' said Mum.

Reluctantly, he held out his arms.

'No, no, you need to take your T-shirt off. And I've brought rope sandals instead of those runners.' She tugged the tunic over his head, tying a cord for a belt around his waist. 'Now off with your shorts,' she ordered.

'Do I have to?' He'd been hitching up his tunic, trying to make it look like a top instead of a dress.

'Yes, they look silly under your costume.'

Perry looked enviously at Dad in his hat, sunglasses and shorts.

'These long sleeves are boiling,' he complained.

'Keep in the shade,' said Mum. 'And put this on your face and legs.' She handed him a tube of sunscreen. 'Melissa, I've brought a parasol for us. It's a Chinese-style one I found in a discount shop, but it looks quite Roman.'

She unfurled a small pink umbrella made from sticks and paper with tassels around the edge.

'Come on,' said Dad. 'Let's find this Roman feast you promised us.'

At the side of the carpark was a large concrete trough.

'Oh,' cried Mum, 'that'll be for the grape-treading. I'll ask when they're doing it.'

In stumbling French, she began to question a man wearing a bright orange 'Information' tag. Perry and Melissa watched her face drop with disappointment.

'They did the treading this morning,' she said. 'We're too late. They've finished now.'

Perry was not a bit surprised. His family was always late.

'We can still eat,' said Dad.

'I can see a pizza oven,' cried Perry, pointing with relief between the marquees. 'Come on.'

'The Romans did not eat pizza,' stated Mum.

Next to the domed oven, a woman was stirring a terracotta pot on some sort of portable barbecue. Mum looked with interest at the evil-looking stew bubbling over the charcoals. The others turned their attention to a man reaching inside the oven with a long-handled paddle. He drew out a round loaf of bread.

'Let's get that,' said Perry.

The loaf had been scored with a knife to make it easy to pull apart. Mum tore off four steaming chunks and handed them around, wrapping each piece in a serviette so it wouldn't burn their fingers.

'Authentic Roman paper napkins!' grinned Melissa.

Perry blew on his piece and took a bite. It tasted like gritty, wholegrain bread.

'It needs something on it,' said Mum. 'I'm going to try *garum*.' She scooped some brown mush out of a clay bowl.

Perry and Melissa looked at each other. 'That's the fish sauce,' whispered Perry.

'It's just like anchovy paste,' said Mum. 'Go on, try it.'

'No way,' said Perry and Melissa together.

'Anchovies are disgusting,' added Melissa.

Up on the stage, a band started to play: a boy thumped a huge tambourine, an old man blew two wooden whistles at the same time, and a young woman twanged away at something with strings.

'Sounds worse than your school band, Perry,' commented Dad.

'That's authentic Roman music,' declared Mum.

Melissa rolled her eyes. 'Mum, let's look at the jewellery stall,' she said.

'Hang on,' said Dad. He pointed at a sign written in French. 'Does that say something about wine-tasting?' he asked.

'Trust you to notice that,' snorted Mum. 'Yes, there are wine tastings in the cellar.'

'I think I'll give it a go,' said Dad. 'Perry, you come too.'

'Perry's underage,' protested Mum.

'In France, kids drink wine, don't they?' said Dad.

Mum frowned. 'One little sip,' she warned.

3

ROMAN TREASURE

'THE ROMANS KEPT THEIR WINE in weird-shaped clay bottles, with handles and pointy bottoms,' said Perry, thinking of the pictures in his book. 'They were called *amphorae*,' he added, pleased he could remember the Latin word.

'I think you've inherited your mother's brain,' said Dad. 'That sounded like one of her tidbits.'

The cellar was underground, down a long flight of stairs. It was cool and dim, the floor made of cobblestones and the ceiling lined with big dark beams. Giant wooden barrels, higher than Dad's head, lay on their sides along the walls.

But, in the centre of the room, a row of ordinary glass wine bottles stood on a counter, and a man – not in Roman costume – waited to pour.

'Which one would Monsieur like to taste first?' he asked.

'Are they all made from local grapes?' asked Dad.

'Of course, Monsieur. All from Château Taradel. We 'ave been making wine 'ere for two thousand years.'

Dad took a sip, held it in his mouth for a moment, then spat into a bowl. Perry noticed that other people around were doing the same.

'Is it really that bad?' he whispered.

Dad chuckled. 'No, that's what you do for wine-tasting,' he explained. 'You just take it in your mouth to taste, then spit it out so you don't get drunk. Here, you have a try.'

He handed Perry a glass of red wine. 'Smell it first,' he instructed.

Perry sniffed it and screwed up his nose. 'I think I'll skip it,' he said, and wandered off to explore.

An old wooden carriage stood on display at the end of the room, but, annoyingly, there were ropes around, blocking it off. Beside it lay a massive sandstone block that was bigger than their coffee table at home. It looked old and worn, and someone had carved grooves and holes in it. What on earth had they used it for? A stone like that must weigh a ton! Puzzled, he crouched down to read the label on it, written in French and English.

Weight from a winch press found in the ruins of the Roman villa, he read. *Holes were added when the villa changed to screw presses around 300 CE. The screw was inserted through the large centre hole and held by a piece of wood fixed with four iron brackets. Eight small holes in the block were used to attach the iron brackets. The ninth hole seems to have been carved by mistake.*

Perry stared at the extra hole. Wow! Seventeen hundred years ago some poor guy made a mistake, and now here it was, sitting on display with a sign on it, for everyone to gawp at!

'But what on earth's a winch press . . . or a screw press?' he muttered.

'Did you say something, honey?' asked a voice.

Perry sprang to his feet, embarrassed. A woman standing in front of a display cabinet was smiling down at him. She had a sheet wound around her.

Mum would not approve of that costume, thought Perry. 'Uh, I said, what's a winch press?' he mumbled.

'Sorry, honey, can't help you there,' she drawled in an American accent. 'But feast your eyes on the treasures in this cabinet. Aren't they just da-arling?'

Perry peered through the glass doors.

He could see cracked clay pots, broken, blackened tools, and lots of corroded bits of metal that might have been pins or coins – or maybe even a ring or bangle. But he couldn't see any sparkling jewels or gold.

'Which ones are the treasures?' he asked.

'Oh, honey, these things are nearly two thousand years old,' gushed the woman. 'They're all *historic* treasures. And they were all buried in that little old ruined villa. Just imagine how those archaeologists felt when they dug them up.'

She swept her arm towards some photos hanging beside the cabinet. They showed people working among the ruins. In one, they were uncovering a mosaic floor. In another, a man in a straw hat was showing a piece of broken pot to the camera.

'If I was younger,' said the woman, 'I'd be down there right now looking for myself. Imagine how it would feel to find something. Well, goodbye, honey, lovely meeting you,' she trilled, and she shuffled away.

Perry stood staring at the photos. The woman was right. It would be fun, digging in the dirt, looking for a bit of old pot or something that the Romans used to use.

'Dad,' he said, running back across the cellar. 'I want to look in that ruin we passed on the way up.'

'Too hot for me out there,' answered Dad. 'Ask Melissa or Mum to go with you.'

Melissa was chatting with a boy – or at least pretending to, as he seemed to be speaking in French – and Mum was in raptures, dipping wool in vats of different coloured dyes.

'Look at these amazing colours,' she exclaimed when Perry turned up beside her. 'All made from roots and leaves. And look: an authentic Roman-style loom!'

Almost hidden behind an eager crowd of weavers, Perry could glimpse a huge wooden frame and long strands of thread.

'I'm waiting for a turn on that!' Mum babbled happily.

Perry sighed. Mum was clearly going to be stuck here for a while.

'Can I go over to the villa?' he asked.

Mum picked up a dripping skein of red wool, and glanced across the vineyard to the ruins.

'All right. Don't stay too long, though. There's no shade over there.'

Perry chose a track through the vineyard. The vines formed low green walls on either side of him, and the grapes clustering among the leaves looked dark and delicious . . .

Just one, he thought.

Pulling a single grape from a bunch, he tossed it in the air and caught it in his mouth, the way he practised with his friends.

Then he bent his head, looking for something he could use for digging. Almost at once, he spotted a thin, dark stick poking out of the ground near the roots of a vine. Crouching down, he tugged it out. It was the size and shape of a pencil, pointed at one end.

He scratched it with his thumbnail, and was startled to see a glint of metal.

Eagerly, he began to scrub at the dirt with the skirt of his tunic. In a moment, the thing lay clean and shiny across his palms.

'Bronze!' he exclaimed, remembering one of Dad's tennis trophies.

He turned it in his fingers, trying to work out what it could be.

Maybe it's one of those pens people used in the olden days, he thought, *the ones they dipped in ink for writing with.*

And then, with a thrill, he knew. He'd seen one just like it in the cabinet only moments ago. The label said it was a stylus, and it was used for scratching words in wax in the days before they had paper and pencils.

He grinned. He hadn't even got down to the ruin yet, and he'd already found a Roman treasure!

4
THE VILLA

PERRY REACHED THE RUIN AND stared around, trying to imagine the villa Mum had described. What had she said? A two-storey mansion with a courtyard, barns, a pigeon tower . . . All he could see now were a few blocks of stone in the ground. It looked more like a plan than a building.

He began to wander through, wishing someone had put up labels to explain what the rooms were. Which were supposed to be the bedrooms? The living room? The kitchen?

One rectangle was bigger than the others, with stumps of columns evenly spaced along three edges of it. When he stepped inside, he could see lines of stones that looked like smaller rooms, opening around it.

'I think I've found the courtyard!' he muttered excitedly.

In a room to his left, someone had protected the floor with a tarpaulin, carefully weighting it down with stones.

Could that be the mosaic under there? he wondered, remembering the photos of the archaeologists digging the ruins.

He hurried towards it, laid his stylus on a low bit of broken wall, and eased up one of the corners.

'Yes!' he cried when he saw the floor underneath.

The tiny squares of coloured stone were dirty, and some were missing, but he could make out the pattern. There was a border that looked like snakes twisting together, and something that might be a flower.

He jumped to his feet, letting the tarpaulin drop again. Maybe the archaeologists hadn't looked everywhere yet. Maybe he could discover another mosaic floor.

Clambering over the broken wall to the next room, he began tearing up the weeds to clear a patch of ground. Then he picked up his stylus. The bronze caught the light, glinting almost like gold. He stopped. The ancient tools in the display cabinet had been discoloured and broken, but this one was shiny and perfect. It seemed a pity to spoil it by digging . . .

He looked down at the ground. Maybe he'd just write with it a bit, and then find something else to dig with.

He patted the earth smooth and began to scratch his name, P . . . E . . . R . . .

He wrote his full name: PEREGRINE, then quickly rubbed out the last E and changed it to PERE-GRINUS. Peregrinus was the name Mum had given him on the plane, a Latin word that meant traveller. If he was using a stylus, he ought to write in Latin.

He started to scratch other words he could remember.

PATER – that was Latin for father.

MATER – mother.

AVE – hello.

A smell of smoke drifted towards him and he glanced up. There was no fire or smoke in sight. He shrugged. *The smell must be coming from the festival*, he thought, and he bent over his writing again.

The sun beat on his head, and the shrilling of cicadas dinned against his ears.

Suddenly, there was a racket of clattering and shouting behind him. Perry shot to his feet. A line of carriages was lumbering between the grape-vines. There were eight mules pulling each one, and people in colourful Roman dress hanging out of the windows, pointing and calling out.

Shoving the stylus in his belt, he hurried towards them, dodging the fallen walls. But as he leapt over the last stone, he almost crashed into a gate – a solid gate, higher than his head. He jerked to a halt and stared. There hadn't been a gate here a second ago! He could still hear the carriages, and the shouting of people on the other side, but all he could see in front of him were thick planks of wood and a towering stone wall. And then he heard the barking of dogs. He spun on his heel.

Two giant black dogs were straining against chains, their feet pawing the air, just metres away from him, and beyond . . .

He let out a gasp. The rocks in the ground seemed to be rising into the air . . . As he stood there, staring, they shaped themselves into walls . . . growing higher and higher . . .

How were they doing this?

It's like a 3D movie, only better! he thought.

In a moment, a whole building had appeared in front of him.

'The mansion!' he breathed.

It had three wings, bordering a courtyard, and a verandah all around the lower floor, with tall columns holding up a red-tiled roof. As he watched, invisible hands seemed to smear the walls with some sort of mortar till they were smooth and white.

Trees rose up inside the courtyard now, starting from their trunks, then spreading out into branches, twigs and leaves. There was a long, red-painted pond in the centre with a stone dolphin trickling water out of its mouth. And then a low wooden fence stretched across the front, with an entrance – *an arbour*, thought Perry, remembering the wooden frame Mum had set up in their own garden, with a few straggly roses growing over it.

A red-haired boy, wearing a costume like Perry's, came hurtling out of the arbour.

'*Tu – demove! Adveniunt,*' he called.

I think that's Latin he's yelling in! thought Perry.

The boy reached him, thrust him aside, and dragged open the gate.

The next moment the carriages came thundering through and Perry had to jump out of the way as the teams of mules came trampling past him, braying and tossing their heads, and the huge wooden wheels with their iron rims almost crushed his toes.

The procession was heading for the arbour, and people came running from every direction to meet it.

Perry and the red-haired boy went running too.

The wheels of the first carriage began to slow, and a man leapt from inside, his amber cloak, pinned at one shoulder, billowing as he jumped. Perry had a glimpse of a purple and white tunic and pale, knitted leggings as the man flung out his arms. A girl and a woman in long robes were rushing towards him.

'*Pater!*' called the girl.

Father! thought Perry. *She's speaking in Latin too.*

The girl looked like one of those Roman mosaics from the museum. She had huge dark eyes and heavy brows, and her hair flowed out behind her in long, brown waves.

As the carriages ground to a halt, the rest of the passengers tumbled out, unloading sacks, boxes and baskets. A man in a short, hooded cape caught Perry by the arm, and shouted in Latin. He gestured at a wooden chest with bronze handles that was resting on the ground.

Perry stared at him. Did the man want him to pick up that big, heavy chest and carry it somewhere?

'*Eia!*' The red-haired boy pushed through the crowd, grabbed a side of the box and jerked his head towards the house.

Perry took the other handle and they staggered together across the cobblestones, through the arbour into the courtyard.

'Who are you ... when you're not standing around like a wet sheep?' panted the boy. 'I'm Carotus.'

'I'm Perry. I mean, Peregrinus. I ... Did you say Carotus? *Carotus!*' Perry burst out laughing, and dropped his end of the box. 'That's clever! You're called Carotus because you've got carrot-coloured hair. And what's his name?' He pointed at a fat man carrying a basket. 'Fatus? And is that one Beardus? And what about him? Is he Shortus?'

His eyes darted to and fro – to the two-storey mansion, to the trees towering over his head . . . the statues, the pond with real-looking water . . .

'How do they do all this?!' he exclaimed. 'Is it some sort of hologram? I didn't know this festival was going to be so cool.'

The redhead looked at him, his mouth hanging open. 'Holy Jupiter, you're crazy,' he said. 'I don't know what you're talking about. And my hair is *not* carrot-coloured.'

Perry grinned and waggled his head. 'Okay, we'll keep on acting,' he said. He hoisted up his end of the box again. 'Where are we taking this thing?'

'To the master's bedroom. Over there.'

As they headed to the far corner of the courtyard, the gravel path crunched realistically under their feet.

I wonder how they do that, thought Perry.

There appeared to be doors opening off the verandah and all of them stood ajar, showing glimpses into different rooms.

'Don't bump the columns,' warned Carotus, manoeuvring the box up a step.

Perry grinned. 'Talk in Latin, remember,' he chided.

'Don't be stupid. I am speaking Latin. And you are too.'

Perry started to laugh. Then stopped. In his head, he repeated the words he had just said: '*Latine loqui, memento.*' He *had* spoken in Latin!

But . . . how on earth had he started understanding, and talking, in Latin?

Bewildered, he missed his footing and fell against a column.

'Ouch,' he grunted, then spun back to gape at the column.

How could he have bumped himself? This was a hologram – wasn't it?

In a daze of confusion, he hardly noticed Carotus pulling him through a door. But the next moment they were in a room, with walls all around them, painted in patterns of red and black, a floor of speckly pink concrete and a smell of flowers . . .

Perry twisted round to stare at a window – a square hole in the wall – as Carotus dragged him across the room. There was a real bee crawling over the sill, and a garden outside with apple trees and bushes of lavender.

'Put it down here,' ordered Carotus, lowering the box at the foot of a bed.

But Perry couldn't move anymore. He was staring around in shock. The villa was not a 3D movie. It was real.

He tried to swallow, and there seemed to be a lump in his throat as big and chunky as one of those stone blocks in the wall. If all this was real, then . . . then somehow, impossibly, the past had come back to life, here on this ruin.

And that meant . . .

He looked at the red-haired boy in front of him.

You're not an actor, thought Perry, *you're* real. *A real boy from seventeen hundred years ago!*

5

THE GIRL WITH THE CAT

'HEY, YOU KNUCKLE-HEAD, I SAID drop the box,' said Carotus.

Shakily, Perry let the chest fall to the floor. The bedhead in front of him was carved in the shape of horses' heads, the bedcover was woven from purple and gold threads, the . . .

I've got to tell Mum! he thought. *She's wasting her time at that festival. There's the real thing right here!*

'*Eia*, where are you going?' demanded Carotus.

'I . . .'

'Turn up the lamp,' said the redhead.

'Lamp?' Perry paused and looked around. He couldn't see a lamp.

'There, on the table,' exclaimed the boy

impatiently, and he pointed at a weird thing made of clay sitting on a small, red-painted table.

Perry took a step towards it. The thing was shaped like a squashed teapot, with a raised design of an eagle and two holes where the lid should have been. He could see a tiny yellow flame flickering inside the spout bit, but how on earth was he supposed to make it glow brighter?

'*Vah*, are you stupid?' snorted Carotus.

He stomped past Perry and snatched up something that looked like a bronze nail lying beside the lamp. He poked it through the spout, then blew on the tiny sputtering flame. It flared up, almost burning off his eyebrows, and he jumped backwards.

Perry smothered a laugh, then the redhead lolloped out of the room, and Perry followed him.

'It's later than I thought,' exclaimed Carotus, jumping down the step to the garden. 'It's nearly dinner hour.'

Perry glanced at the sun still glaring in the sky.

You Romans eat dinner early! he thought. *It's still only afternoon.*

But Carotus was looking at the ground, not the sky.

'How are you telling the time?' asked Perry curiously.

'By that, of course,' said Carotus, pointing at his long shadow. 'How do *you* tell the time?'

'Er, I guess I can't,' Perry admitted. Well, he couldn't ... not if he didn't have a watch or a phone.

Carotus rolled his eyes. 'Of course you can't,' he said. 'Here ... Can you pick flowers?' He grabbed a basket off a stone bench and crouched by a flowerbed.

Perry hesitated, then knelt down beside him. He would go and get his family in a little while.

'Pick the marigolds,' said Carotus, breaking off some bright, orangey-yellow flowers and dropping them in the basket. 'It's going to be a special dinner,' he said, 'to celebrate the master coming home.'

Perry looked at him nervously. A special dinner ... He hoped they wouldn't have to eat mice!

To his surprise, Carotus stopped picking flowers, and started inspecting the leaves.

'What are you looking for?' asked Perry.

Carotus chuckled. 'You'll see.'

A few minutes later, the redhead gave a shout of triumph and stood up. 'Come on, off to the dining room. Got to get there before Gabrina. She's the housekeeper,' he explained. 'Mean old cow-face.'

They sped along the verandah, and Perry just had time to glimpse a little shrine with statues of gods glittering in the sunlight, before they were charging through an entrance hall and up to the door of a large, ornate room.

How is this a dining room? wondered Perry as he followed Carotus inside.

It had no dining table or chairs, just a circular coffee table with a curved couch sweeping halfway around it. A woman was lazing on the couch, fanning herself with an ivory and gold fan. She had a very pale face and was dressed in a long, sea-green robe with matching wrap.

'That's Donata, the mistress,' whispered Carotus.

'Valentia,' they heard her say, 'come and sit down instead of crawling on the floor like a slave.'

There was a faint tinkling sound, then a girl rose from behind the couch. She had big brown eyes and dark, arching brows. *That's the girl I saw running to meet the carriages*, Perry realised. *The girl with the long, flowing hair.*

But now her hair was pulled back in a bun and she was dressed in a full-length rusty-coloured robe with trailing sleeves. Dangling from each wrist was a charm bracelet that tinkled as she moved.

She shot Perry a curious look. Then her gaze swept past him to Carotus, and she smiled broadly. 'Carotus, look what my father's brought from up north!' she said.

At that moment an animal padded out from behind the couch. It was the fattest cat Perry had ever seen – a furry ball covered with tiger stripes of dark brown and white.

Valentia swished her long sleeve in the cat's face, but the animal just squeezed its eyes and yawned.

'You lazy thing,' murmured the girl, bending to run her fingers through its fur.

'Valentia,' drawled the woman again, 'that creature should not be in our dining room. Your father brought it for catching mice. Carotus, take it out to the barn.'

When the girl pouted in disappointment, the redhead winked at her, and the next moment he and the cat were chasing around the room, leaping over stools and diving under tables, and Valentia was rolling around, giggling.

'Carotus!' said Donata sharply.

Perry saw Carotus throw Valentia an apologetic glance as he caught the cat and carried it, struggling, through the doorway.

Donata turned her gaze on Perry. 'So, you're one of the new slaves brought from up north,' she said.

Perry stared back at her. Was that why no one was surprised he was here? But . . . a *slave?!*

Thanks for making me a slave costume, Mum, he thought wryly.

'I trust you will be less vexing than young Carotus,' Donata continued, rising from the couch.

Ha! So Carotus was a slave too.

'Valentia, I am just going to put on those emerald earrings your father brought me,' said Donata. 'He will be coming in for dinner at any moment. Boy . . .' She waved her hand at Perry. 'Do the flowers.' And she, too, left the room.

Perry took a step to follow. This was his chance to fetch his family. But then he stopped. It'd be fun to pretend to be a slave, just for a bit . . .

6

SLAVE

THERE WAS A SILVER JUG standing on a tall side table. Perry crossed the room, feeling Valentia's eyes following him. The bronze legs of the table had big, bulging lions' heads glaring out of them, and the marble top was almost as high as his chin. He lifted down the heavy jug and peeked inside. Yes, it had water in it. Placing the jug next to his basket on the floor, he took out a few flowers and began to push their stems through the narrow neck of the jug.

There was a sputter of laughter behind him.

'That warm water's not for flowers. It's for drinking, silly,' exclaimed Valentia.

He blushed as he turned to look up at her.

She was standing, leaning against the couch, her big dark eyes sparkling with laughter.

'Can you understand me?' she asked. 'Do you speak Latin? Or . . . or Greek? Or . . . What do they speak up north? Barbarian?'

'I speak Latin,' he muttered.

'Well, put them around like this.' She came over to his side, yanked the flowers out of the jug, twisted a few together and draped them across the crimson cushions of the couch. 'See? Doesn't that look pretty? Don't they do that where you come from?'

'Er, no.'

'Well, that's what you do here.' She tipped her head on one side and looked at him curiously again. 'I wonder why Father brought you all the way from Augusta Treverorum. What's your name?'

'Perry . . . Peregrinus.'

'I'm Valentia,' she said. 'I'm nearly eleven. How old are you?'

'Eleven.'

There was a stirring in the hallway outside and a short, cross-looking woman came barging into the room, squinting from side to side.

Carotus followed her, carrying a platter of food. He caught Perry's eye, and grimaced behind the woman's back.

That must be Gabrina, the grumpy housekeeper, thought Perry.

Behind Carotus came a little girl. She was staggering under the weight of a huge platter, much too big for her. She looked only seven or eight years old.

'Ooh, what have we got to eat?' cried Valentia, rushing to meet them.

Perry ran forward too.

'Snails,' beamed Valentia, looking at Carotus's dish.

Snails! Yuck! thought Perry. 'What are those?' he asked, pointing at three little humps on the girl's plate.

The girl flicked him a shy glance. 'Pigeons in mustard and fig sauce,' she whispered.

Eww! That's almost as bad as mice, thought Perry.

The girl crashed her load onto a small table near the door.

'No, Rittia,' snapped Gabrina. 'Put it on the dining table, you silly girl!'

But there isn't a dining table, thought Perry.

Then he saw Carotus head for the low table in front of the couch. That must be what they used for dining.

Little Rittia struggled to pick up her heavy plate again.

'Here, I'll help,' offered Perry.

'Leave her!' snarled grumpy Gabrina. 'There's no room around here for slaves who are weaklings. And you – fetch your own dish.'

She jerked her chin at the door, but Perry stood gaping at her. He remembered Mum saying there were dozens of slaves at the villa, but he hadn't imagined they'd be little kids like Rittia!

Carotus gave him a kick. 'Get the plate,' he muttered, 'before . . .'

'Boy!' roared Gabrina.

Perry jumped to obey her.

A man was hovering in the hallway, holding out another plate.

Why can't the guy just bring it in himself? Perry wondered.

But he reached to take it. Maybe different slaves had different jobs.

The plate, made of silver, had a raised border of lions and leopards, and it was piled high with all sorts of unrecognisable food.

I hope slaves don't eat this stuff, thought Perry as he lowered it to the dining table.

Carotus leaned across and pointed at the small, pale-yellow root vegetables swimming around in an oily sauce with little green specks in it.

'Peregrinus, those are carrots,' he said.

Yellow carrots! No wonder Carotus had insisted his hair wasn't carrot-coloured.

They're more like the colour of my own hair, thought Perry.

'Valentia,' boomed a cheery voice from the doorway.

It was the man who had leapt from the first carriage. Perry recognised the tanned face, curly dark hair and beard, but now he was dressed in a loose, long-sleeved tunic of honey brown, with large black and white circles woven in the skirt and shoulders.

He strode towards Valentia and caught her by the elbows. 'My daughter, what a lovely young lady you have grown into,' he exclaimed. Then he wrapped her in a hug. 'When I left, you were just a little girl.'

Valentia leaned against his chest. 'Father, I'm so happy you're home,' she murmured.

Donata came hurrying into the room, fancy green earrings dangling from her ears. 'Ah, Maximus, let's eat,' she cried. 'You must be hungry after your hours of travel.'

'Rittia, fetch the bowl and pitcher for washing,' hissed Gabrina. 'Carotus, take the wine, and you ...' She shoved the jug of drinking water at Perry. 'You serve this.'

I can do that, thought Perry. *And it's better than eating pigeons and snails.*

Valentia drew up a stool to the table, but the master and mistress stretched out on the big, curved couch, each resting on an elbow.

They're going to eat lying down! thought Perry.

Sure enough, resting on one elbow, Maximus leaned across and plunged his free hand right into the serving dish of pigeons. Perry watched, astonished, as the bird was lifted, dripping, from the sauce, and Maximus tore at the flesh with his teeth, dropping the tiny bones on the floor.

Donata and Valentia did the same.

No plates! thought Perry. *And no knives or forks!*

When they finished the pigeons, Rittia poured water over their sticky fingers, struggling to hold the silver washing bowl underneath.

Then Maximus reached for the dish of walnuts.

'Father,' exclaimed Valentia, 'when I was little, didn't you used to crack those for me with your bare hands?'

Smiling, Maximus clasped two of the nuts in one fist and squeezed. *Crunch.* He unfurled his fingers.

'Yes, like that!' cried Valentia, reaching in to find the bits of nut in the broken shells.

Perry felt a nudge in his ribs.

'Sleepy-head,' whispered Carotus. 'Get to work. I'll pour the wine, then you do the water.' And he marched towards the diners with a smirk on his face.

What's so funny? wondered Perry.

There were three wine goblets of greenish glass set out on the table.

Wine for Valentia too! thought Perry.

He watched Carotus begin to fill them.

'Come on, add the water,' prompted the redhead.

'On – on top of the wine?' whispered Perry.

'Of course!'

When Perry reached Valentia, he stared at a fat green caterpillar swimming around in her wine. Did Romans drink caterpillars as well as eating snails and mice?

He glanced at Carotus. The redhead was sniggering, watching Valentia pick up her glass.

It's a prank, thought Perry, *and . . .*

'Hey . . .' he burst out as Valentia nearly took a sip.

Valentia hesitated, peeked in her glass, and glared at Carotus.

The next instant, Perry found himself being growled at by Gabrina.

'Silence,' she scolded in a low, angry voice. 'Don't you know how to behave properly in the dining room?'

Valentia sent him a look of sympathy but Perry just shrugged. It didn't matter what the grumpy housekeeper thought of him. He wasn't really a slave, and the first chance he got, he was going to slip outside and find his family.

Over on the couch, Maximus let out a loud, contented sigh. 'Ah, it's good to be home at last.' He sucked the flesh from a snail and tossed the shell on the floor. 'Nothing tastes as well as the produce of my own farm. Speaking of produce, dear, Salutus says the grapes are ready for picking. The men will start in the morning.'

Perry saw Valentia and Carotus glance at each other excitedly.

'Heavens, husband, it is fortunate you arrived home today then, in time for the harvest,' replied Donata. 'Now, have you finished the first course, dear? Shall we make the prayer offering?'

When Maximus nodded, she turned to Carotus and Peregrinus. 'Boys, we need some fresh garlands on the shrine,' she said.

The shrine! thought Perry. *This is my chance!*

He remembered the shrine was just outside the door. He'd seen it on the verandah . . .

As soon as Carotus began to move, Perry took off, rushing past him out of the room.

7

CEREMONY

LEAPING OFF THE VERANDAH, PERRY made a dash for the arbour. He could hear Carotus calling out behind.

'*Eia!*' shouted the slave boy. 'Where are you going?'

'Just across the vineyard,' Perry flung over his shoulder. 'To the festival. I'll be back . . .'

Footsteps came pounding after him. 'You idiot,' shouted Carotus. 'Stop!'

When Perry burst through the arbour, the guard dogs leapt up, barking.

'Quiet!' ordered Carotus.

Perry had just reached the gate and wrenched it open, when Carotus came bounding up to him, and grabbed hold of his sleeve. 'What . . . the Jupiter . . . are you talking about?' he panted.

'The festival,' cried Perry again.

'What festival?' demanded Carotus.

'There!' Perry turned and flung out an arm.

Then he felt as if someone had thrown him in a frozen pool, and he was crashing through the ice . . .

There was no château, no marquee, no crowd of people. Just grapevines, as far as he could see.

'What festival?' Carotus demanded again.

'I . . . Where's it gone?' croaked Perry.

Carotus rolled his eyes. 'It was never there,' he said. 'You're crazy. Now, come on, we have to make the garlands for the shrine. Hurry.'

But Perry clung to the gate, staring across the vineyard. If the festival wasn't there, then . . . then what had happened to his family? What had happened to his own world – and how was he going to get back to it?!

'Come on, they're waiting for us!'

In a daze, Perry let the redhead drag him away from the gate. On the other side of the arbour, Carotus took something from his belt, unfolded it, and began to slash at the ivy. Then he grabbed some pink flowers off a bush.

'Come on, hurry,' he called, running towards the verandah.

Perry threw a last, desperate glance at the gate, then turned to follow.

Carotus was twisting strands of ivy into a chain in front of the shrine.

'Hold this one,' he said, 'and put the roses in.' He thrust a couple of flowers at Perry too.

'Ow, they've got thorns,' Perry complained.

'Of course they do. They're roses!'

Perry looked at the flowers and leaves. 'I don't . . .' he mumbled.

Carotus glanced up. '*Vah*, don't you know how to make garlands either?'

Perry just stared at the leafy thing hanging from his hands. All he could think about was the vanished festival.

Carotus snatched it back from him, finished the garlands and draped them over the god statues.

'There,' he said. 'Now come on, they'll be waiting for us.'

In the dining room, Maximus and his wife were just rising from the table.

'Slaves, bring the silverware,' ordered Maximus, and he strutted out of the room.

As Donata and Valentia followed him, Gabrina turned to the cupboard and unlocked it with a large iron key. Inside was a glittering array of jugs, bowls, plates and boxes, all made from silver.

'Carotus . . .' Gabrina placed a round, flat bowl in his hands. 'You take the offering dish, and I'll bring the incense.' She glanced at Perry and Rittia. 'Rittia, you stick with the washing things, and you, new boy, can I trust you to hold the wine?'

Before Perry could reply, he was holding a tall, thin jug, and Gabrina was shooing them out of the room.

'Quiet!' she warned.

Silently and solemnly, they paraded across the hallway and onto the verandah.

Maximus, Donata and Valentia were gathered in front of the shrine. A little fire in the middle sent a flickering red light dancing on their faces.

As Rittia stepped towards them with her washing bowl, Perry turned to gaze across the courtyard. It was twilight now. The fence and open gate were just black silhouettes beyond the arbour. And beyond them . . . a greyness seemed to stretch far, far into nothingness. Was his own world still out there – somewhere?

How am I going to find my family again? he thought worriedly.

A smell of incense drifted from the shrine and he turned back.

The master had the silver offering dish in his hands. He swung to face Perry, and held the empty dish towards him. Perry stared.

There was a long pause.

'Pour in some wine,' hissed Carotus.

Hastily, Perry tilted the jug he was holding, but he'd barely started when Maximus swivelled away.

Perry just managed to straighten the jug in time. Maximus let a few drops fall on the flames. Then, with hands raised, palms upwards, he began to pray:

'Jupiter, god of thunder, and the ancestral spirits of this household who protect us,' he said, 'I offer thanks for returning me safely home.'

Perry looked back towards the gate again. *What about me?* he thought. *How am* I *going to get home?*

8

IN THE KITCHEN

'FINISHED AT LAST!' CAROTUS SANG OUT.

The last pigeon bone had been picked clean, and the last plum stone tossed on the floor. The family had finally finished their dinner and left the dining room.

'Our turn now!' beamed little Rittia, picking up the dish with remnants of cottage cheese and honey smeared around it.

'Off to the kitchen!' hooted Carotus, grabbing the leftover salted dates, and the peaches stewed in some sort of smelly sauce.

Laughing and chattering, they followed Gabrina through the dining room door.

'Come on, Peregrinus,' called Carotus.

But Perry stared after the disappearing slaves in

dismay. They were taking those disgusting scraps to eat for themselves! He seemed to hear Melissa's voice again as if she was right beside him. 'We're about to have a Roman feast, remember . . .'

Melissa, you should have seen the real dinner, he thought. *Eels, snails, pigeons . . . And now I've got to eat what's left of it!*

He imagined his big sister lounging on the dining couch in her long pink costume with her dangly bead earrings. If she was here, she would have fitted right in with the family. No one would have mistaken *her* for a slave.

And if you were here, Melissa, he thought, *you'd know how to get us home again. You'd find the way on your phone!*

He almost laughed as he blinked back tears, then he realised the voices of the slaves were fading in the distance.

'Wait!' he shouted, and rushed towards the door.

He couldn't lose Carotus! Then he'd really be alone.

He burst onto the verandah, jumped down the step, and looked wildly around. Where had they gone? They'd said they were heading for the kitchen, but where was the kitchen? Doors stood open all around the verandah, but he couldn't see anything that looked like a room for cooking in.

He began to run, charging past the beds of roses and marigolds, past the fountain, past a naked statue of a goddess.

At last he heard the others again – and saw them moving – on the other side of the arbour. They were turning right, heading for a gate in a high fence.

The house is back there, he thought. *Why are they going this way?*

He hurtled after them and found himself in another yard. But this was not a pretty courtyard with a garden. This was a working yard. It had big, lumpy pebbles for paving, buildings of odd shapes and sizes dotted around the sides, and even a twig broom, like a witch's broom, propped against one wall.

Smoke wafted from a small white building on his left, and Rittia was just vanishing through the door.

Could this building out here be the kitchen?

He rushed after her, then stopped in the doorway. All he could see in the murky interior was a cluster of shadowy, stooped figures, and something red glowing in a corner.

A man broke away and strode towards him. The man's tunic was smudged with a pale flour-like dust that wafted around him as he moved. He clapped a hand on Perry's shoulder.

'You must be another new slave from up north,' said the man. 'Come, eat with us.'

As Perry was drawn forward, he spotted Gabrina seated grandly at the head of a large, crowded table – *A normal height table!* thought Perry – while Carotus and Rittia sat on the other side, already stuffing their faces with food.

The redhead grinned at him. 'Decided you were hungry, did you?' He thrust a wooden three-legged stool against Perry's legs. 'You can sit here,' he said.

Perry sat, but there seemed to be nowhere to fit his knees. The table was a silly design, with a rail running all the way around the table legs.

'Carotus, introduce us to this new slave,' requested the man.

'He's called Peregrinus,' said Carotus. 'But he doesn't know anything. He . . . he's about as useful as a second tail on a dog!'

He laughed at his own joke, and several people joined in.

'Tut, tut, Carotus,' scolded a high-pitched voice.

It came from an ancient, tubby little man, with a bald spot on the top of his head and a fringe of grey curls. He had a round face, scrunched up around a little bubble of a nose.

'Remember the morals we write in our lessons,' he quavered. '*Ridicule no one. Despise not your inferior. Never pass judgement . . .*'

He waggled his finger, and Carotus nudged Perry in the ribs.

'This old bore,' he said, 'used to be tutor to the master. His name is Balbus. He gives lessons to Valentia now. And me too, when I turn up.'

Perry looked at him in surprise. Were slaves allowed to go to school?

'And I,' said the dusty man, 'am unlucky enough to be this rude boy's grandfather. My name is Poppillus.'

Carotus didn't look the least ashamed. 'Grandfather's an important slave,' he said. 'He bakes the bread!'

'Speaking of bread ...' Poppillus broke off a piece and offered it.

'Thank you!' gasped Perry.

The bread looked just like the wholegrain loaf from the festival.

'Dip it in this,' offered a woman on the other side of him.

Perry turned. A toddler on the woman's lap was paddling his fingers in a large clay bowl. The baby raised a fistful of lumpy, yellowy-coloured muck, and slurped it into his mouth.

'Er ...' said Perry, as the woman pushed the bowl towards him.

'It's barley porridge,' she said encouragingly.

Carotus took the hunk of bread from Perry's fingers and scooped some porridge onto it.

'Here,' he said.

Reluctantly, Perry took a bite. The porridge was lukewarm, lumpy and slimy, and it seemed as if everyone else had been dipping in it too.

'Needs garum,' said Carotus, reaching for another bowl.

Perry caught a whiff of the smell, and clapped his hand to his nose. Real garum stank worse than the stinkiest sweaty socks in the world!

'I don't like garum,' he croaked, trying not to breathe.

'Everyone likes garum.'

'Not me!'

Carotus dipped his own bread in garum and began to munch it, watching Perry curiously.

Perry looked around to see what else he could eat. The leftovers from the dining room had been tipped off their silver platters onto orange clay dishes and most of them looked even more unappetising now. He chose a raw plum and ate it, looking around the room.

Through the smoky haze he made out something that must be the stove – a stone bench with embers of a fire glowing red in the top of it. A woman was stirring a sooty clay pot balanced on an iron tripod over the heat. Beside her, two clay amphorae were propped against the wall, their pointed bases resting on the floor.

They're huge, much bigger than I imagined, thought Perry. They were almost as big as he was. What could be stored inside them? Maybe oil for cooking?

Carotus finished his smelly meal and reached for a plum too.

'Who are all these people?' Perry asked, indicating the men, women and children crammed around the table.

'Well, you know those two, of course,' said Carotus, nodding at the men dressed, despite the warm weather, in scarves and long, heavy woollen tunics. 'They're the carpenters who travelled from up north with you. Aren't they?' He gave Perry a piercing look.

Perry felt his cheeks go red. 'What about all the others?' he said quickly.

Carotus started to point around the table to each person in turn, reeling off their weird names. 'He's Tiluvimpus, the water-carrier.' Tiluvimpus was hunched over his food, eating without speaking to anyone, but next to him, a little boy smiled and waved. He looked about seven years old. 'That's Gabrina's grandson, Lollius. He runs messages. And that's Bonica . . .' He indicated a girl about Melissa's age. 'She's Donata's personal maid. And that . . .' He pointed to a smiling lady in a seat opposite them. '. . . is Habita, my mother.'

Perry stared at Habita. She was wearing a small, stiff headscarf and . . . *Her dress is just like my Mum's*, he thought, remembering the blue dress with broad yellow stripes his mother had worn for the festival. *Mum would be so glad to see she got it right.* He blinked hard. *If only she was here . . . If only my whole family was here!*

But now, all the slaves were getting up and starting to leave the table. As Carotus rose, he turned questioningly to Perry.

'Where are you going to sleep?' he asked.

Sleep?! Perry stared at him. *I don't want to sleep here!* He looked around the gloomy room, filled with smoke, strange smells, and people he didn't know. *I want to be back in Arles with my family,* he thought, with a sick, tight feeling in his stomach, *safe and comfortable in my hotel bed, not here, in this strange place!*

9

NIGHT TIME

'YOU CAN SHARE WITH ME and Grandfather if you want,' offered Carotus. 'All the new slaves will be sleeping wherever they can.'

'Thank you,' whispered Perry.

It was growing dark when they stepped outside, and the buildings were just pale shapes at the edges of the workyard. Perry looked around.

'Er . . . is there a toilet I can use?' he asked.

'Of course,' said Carotus, stopping beside the kitchen. 'The slave latrines are in here.'

He reached for the door, and Perry squeezed his eyes shut. *Please,* he prayed, *don't let it be one of those share-toilets, like they had in that book on the Romans.*

But it was! When he opened one eye to peek, he saw a woman in there already – sitting on a long wooden seat with three holes in it for three people to use at the same time.

He spun away in embarrassment.

'I thought you needed to go,' said Carotus, when he and the woman strolled out again.

'I . . . I'll go in now,' stammered Perry.

He dashed inside, trying to be as fast as he could. There was no toilet paper, of course, but standing in a wooden basin of water, just like in the book, was a stick with a sponge on the end.

I'm going to die of some awful disease, thought Perry.

He burst from the room again, and looked around.

The redhead was nowhere in sight.

'*Carotus!*' hissed Perry.

He peered into the shadows.

'Carotus?' he called again.

With a shout of laughter, Carotus leapt into view. He'd been hiding behind a mound of something.

'You thought I'd left you, didn't you?' he sniggered. 'Come on.'

Perry hurried to keep up, stumbling on the large rounded paving stones. As they passed the front of the villa, the loud snarling of the guard dogs sounded from the darkness ahead.

'Don't worry, they're still chained up,' called Carotus. 'Probably,' he added, his teeth glinting in a grin.

He ran off through the shadows, and a moment later, the noise stopped.

Perry crept forward. A small, two-storey building came into view, and there were the dogs, with Carotus patting and soothing them. Perry stared. Their massive black heads had manes like lions, and, at the sight of him, they burst into loud barks again.

'Quiet, Lupa! Down, Killer!' ordered Carotus.

The guard dogs lay down, but their ears went on twitching and they let out little growling sounds as Perry edged closer.

Carotus gestured at the top floor of the building. 'That's where Gabrina lives,' he said, 'and Beratius the farm manager. And their families.' He pushed open the front door. 'And here,' he said, 'is where Grandfather and I sleep. Off the bakery.'

They stepped through, and the heavy wooden door thudded behind them.

They were standing in a large room with a huge wood-fired oven against the wall. Poppillus was mixing dough with two other slaves at a stone bench. He waved at them with a floury hand.

'I told Peregrinus he can sleep with us,' Carotus called.

'Don't stay up late chatting, then,' warned his grandfather. 'Remember, you'll have an early start in the morning for the grape harvest!'

'I won't forget that!' Carotus sang out.

The boys crossed to the far end of the hall and Carotus thrust open a door to reveal a small bedroom with two single beds on a floor of beaten earth.

'You can sleep there,' he said, pointing at the narrow straw mat under their feet.

Perry thought of the bed Mum made when his friends came to stay – a blow-up double with two proper pillows and a soft, comfy doona.

Suddenly, he had an image of Carotus's mum, in her blue dress, sitting at the kitchen table.

'Where's your mum?' he demanded. Surely any mother could find him a better bed than this . . .

'She sleeps in the villa, in Valentia's room,' said Carotus, dropping onto the nearest bed.

'Valentia's room? Why?' asked Perry, puzzled.

'Because . . .' Carotus lifted one foot to his knee, and loosened the leather lace. 'Mum is Valentia's nursemaid.'

'But . . . isn't Valentia that girl we saw in the dining room?' asked Perry. 'She's nearly eleven! What does she need a nursemaid for?'

'Mum dresses her, does her hair, washes her, all that stuff. And then sleeps in her room in case Valentia needs her during the night,' said Carotus. 'Valentia doesn't do anything for herself. She's the master's daughter.'

Shucking off his sandals, the slave boy kicked them across the room so they thudded one by one against the wall.

'Carotus,' called Poppillus, 'was that you throwing your shoes about?'

Carotus grinned and poked his tongue in the direction of the doorway. Then he pulled something from his belt and opened it.

'Bet you haven't got a folding knife like this,' he said.

'Er . . . no,' said Perry.

It had a tiny metal blade and a handle made of something that looked like bone.

Then, with a start, Perry remembered what he did have. He clapped his hand to his waist. Yes, it was still there.

Beaming, Carotus closed his knife again. Laying it on top of his wooden bedhead, he flopped down, and pulled up his cover.

'The grape harvest is fun,' he said. 'Last year I only got to sort grapes, but now I'll be big enough to help with the cutting. I'm nearly twelve, you know.'

Abruptly, he sat up again, and pointed at a large clay bowl under his grandfather's bed. 'There's the piss-pot to use for a toilet in the night.' He gave a loud yawn, lay down, and rolled away from Perry onto his other side.

'You'd better ... move your mat ... from the door,' he mumbled, 'so Grandfather doesn't tread on you when he comes in.'

But Perry waited, rigid with excitement, till it sounded as if the redhead had fallen asleep. Then, with a trembling hand, he drew the stylus from his belt.

This is it! he thought. *This is the key!*

It had to be this old Roman tool that had stolen him from his own time. He remembered kneeling among the ruins, scratching words in the dirt ... and then, the next moment, that mysterious smell of smoke, the walls rising out of the ground ...

So all I have to do is write with it again, he thought, *only in English this time. When I wrote words in Latin, I came here. So if I write words in English, I'll go back again ...*

10

THE NAME
ON THE COFFIN

DROPPING TO HIS KNEES, PERRY stabbed the tip of the stylus in the earth floor, and scraped through the dirt with deep, fierce strokes.

HELLO PERRY, he scrawled, and then the names of his family. Eagerly, he raised his head.

The soft light of an oil lamp flickered through the room; and Carotus still slept in the bed in front of him.

It hadn't worked!

Gripping the stylus tighter, he leaned closer to the ground. *Think!* he told himself. *Those weren't the right words.*

COMPUTER, he tried next. TELEPHONE,

INTERNET, MICROWAVE, CAR ... Each time he scratched a new word, he glanced up, but each time the room remained unchanged.

He grew more and more impatient. TV, he scribbled, ELECTRICITY, FRIDGE, NANA, GRANDPA. He listed the names of his friends, the names of footy teams ... but nothing worked.

And then he heard one of the bakers call, 'Sleep tight,' in the big hall, and the soft *pad-pad* of leather-soled shoes approaching the bedroom.

Quickly, Perry wrenched the mat across the churned-up floor, shoved the stylus underneath, and flung himself down, closing his eyes.

Just in time.

He heard the door creak open, footsteps crossing the room, a pause, then the loud *hiss* of the old man using the toilet pot.

Through closed eyelids, Perry sensed the room grow darker.

Poppillus must be putting out the lamp, he thought.

At last came the creaking and rustling of someone climbing into bed, and then the slow, deep rumble of snores.

Cautiously, Perry opened his eyes. The room was pitch black. *No-o*, now he was stuck here for the rest of the night!

I just needed one more minute, he thought crossly.

He heaved onto his side, and stared at the darkness, planning what words he'd write as soon as he got a chance in the morning.

Maybe he'd list all the things in his bedroom, or . . . had he tried MUM and DAD yet? He couldn't remember.

If I was home now, he thought, *Dad would be sitting on my bed talking footy; and Mum* . . . He gulped. *Mum would be coming in, saying it was time to go to sleep, giving me a goodnight kiss . . .*

Tears prickled his eyes and he hastily flung himself on his back.

Think of something else, he told himself.

A wobbly smile crept onto his face as he imagined telling his family about today. They'd never believe he'd been to real Roman times, but he'd tell them anyway – about slimy barley porridge, and garum that was really stinky, and lamps that looked like teapots.

And about Carotus who dropped caterpillars in people's wineglasses, and Valentia, the master's daughter, who had a nursemaid to do everything for her . . .

She's not that stuck-up, though, he decided, thinking of the way she giggled, and how upset she'd looked when Gabrina growled at him . . .

Valentia . . . Where had he heard that name before?

He closed his eyes, trying to forget the hard, cold mat, trying to pretend he was in bed at home.

Valentia, he thought drowsily. *It's a pretty name. Maybe it's a song.*

Then his eyes shot open. He remembered where he'd come across it before. It was the other name on that coffin, the name of the girl who'd died when she was eleven years, two months and one day old. He could see it, engraved in the stone: Camilla Valentia.

But . . .

He sat bolt upright. Valentia had told him she was nearly eleven. That meant – if she was the girl from the coffin – she was about to die in a couple of months!

But it couldn't be her, he told himself, *there must be hundreds of Valentias. Surely, she couldn't be the same one. If her name was Camilla Valentia, people would call her Camilla, wouldn't they? They wouldn't call her by her second name.*

He lay down and closed his eyes again; and this time, exhausted, he dropped off to sleep.

11

THE GRAPE HARVEST

'IT'S THE GRAPE HARVEST TODAY!'

Perry was vaguely aware of footsteps thudding past him and the sound of a door crashing open. He sat up, blinking, and looked around. He could smell fresh bread. And there, in the next room, was the strange sight of men shovelling loaves from a huge, wood-fired oven ... and a red-haired boy standing by a front door, gazing out.

Memories of the day before came flooding in.

'They've started already,' cried Carotus, spinning away from the door and running back. 'Peregrinus,' he yelled, 'get up! This is the best time of the whole year and you're missing out. Come on! They're harvesting the grapes and soon they'll be stomping them in the treading pit.'

He scrambled for his sandals, tied them on, snatched up his folding knife and flew out of the room.

Quickly, Perry felt under the mat and drew out his stylus. The bakers were putting more bread in the oven. They wouldn't notice him scribbling.

Pressing the bronze tip in the earth floor, he began to write: M ... U ...

But then he stopped. The words Carotus had shouted were still ringing in his head:

The best time of the whole year, and you're missing out!

Yesterday, he'd missed the grape-treading because they'd arrived at the festival too late. He wasn't going to miss out again.

He straightened up, lifting the stylus from the floor.

I'll just stay a bit longer, he decided.

Shoving the stylus in his belt, he grabbed his sandals.

His family would be frantic – they'd have police all over the world searching for him – but still ... they'd be okay when he turned up again.

And imagine Mum's face when I tell her all the things I've seen!

As he hurried through the next room, Carotus's grandfather glanced up and smiled at him. 'Here,' he called, tossing a hunk of bread.

'Thank you,' cried Perry, leaping to catch it. It was almost too hot to eat.

'You'll find Carotus down among the grape-vines,' said the baker.

'I know,' Perry grinned, remembering how excited the redhead had been the night before, talking about cutting the grapes.

The guard dogs set up a vicious barking as he stepped outside, but Perry ignored them and dashed past. At the gate to the vineyard, he paused, gazing at the scene in front of him.

All down the long rows of vines, men were chopping at grapes. He could see the *flash flash* of knife blades catching the sunlight, and the long, cone-shaped baskets slung on their backs. The vines were taller than modern ones. The pickers had to stretch up high. He watched as they swung their arms, chopped the clusters of purple fruit, dropped them in their baskets, and swung again. It was almost like a dance.

Then he hurried between the vines, searching for a splash of red hair among the pickers.

There was none in the first row . . . or the next.

Where was Carotus?

A boy about Melissa's age came whistling past, leading a donkey cart. The cart was piled high with baskets of grapes.

'Hello,' called Perry, 'do you know where Carotus is?'

'In the pressing room,' replied the boy, jerking his chin in the direction he was heading.

Confused, Perry looked back at the vines. Carotus had been so sure he was going to help with the picking, but . . .

'Wait!' he pleaded, and spurted forward to catch up with the boy and the donkey. 'Where's the pressing room?'

'Just follow this load,' said the boy. He gave Perry a curious look. 'You don't seem to know much,' he said. 'Are you one of the new slaves from up north?'

'Er, yes,' mumbled Perry.

'What's your name? I'm Abalus.'

'I'm Peregrinus.'

'Well, Peregrinus, they're just waiting for this load to start the treading,' said Abalus. 'Have you ever seen grape-treading before?'

'No,' answered Perry.

'City boy, are you?'

'Yes!'

Abalus gave a yank at the donkey's bridle. 'Come on, hurry up, you lazy ears,' he urged.

Skirting the front gate, they passed chickens cackling in a hen run, and pale, hairless pigs snuffling in a pigsty. They circled a tall white tower, with hundreds of pigeons cooing and wheeling through little holes in the top.

That's where the cook got the pigeons for dinner last night, realised Perry, staring up at them.

Then they swung through a gate into a cobbled yard.

'I know where we are!' Perry exclaimed.

There on the right was the kitchen where he'd been the night before. He glanced at the smoke drifting out the door, and wondered why the Romans had never thought of chimneys.

The next instant a crowd of people came rushing from the building beyond, shouting in excitement.

'They're here! The next load's arrived!'

Men, dressed in nothing but strips of cloth around their hips, reached in to haul out the baskets. Perry found himself caught up in the crowd as they surged around the cart, then swept him along with them into the building.

He stumbled through the double doors and saw the men lifting the baskets high with their big, bare, muscly arms, and sending streams of dark, glistening grapes pouring over a long wooden benchtop.

And there, at last, Perry spotted Carotus. He was standing at the bench among a string of women.

'What are you doing here?' Perry gasped out,

pushing his way to Carotus's side. 'Why aren't you picking the grapes?'

The slave boy pulled a face. 'They said I'm still not big enough,' he growled. 'And I'm nearly twelve!'

'Who are you?' snapped a woman at Perry's other side.

He turned. It was the woman he'd seen in the toilet last night – the one who'd been sitting on one of the holes when he'd wanted to go. He felt himself blush scarlet, but she didn't seem at all embarrassed.

'Hurry up and make yourself useful,' she said, without waiting for his answer.

Perry looked around. Everyone was taking bunches of grapes from the bench, pulling bits off, then tossing the bunches into a large basket behind them.

'Do you know what to do?' demanded toilet woman.

'Er . . . no.'

'Look for anything that might spoil the wine,' she said, 'leaves left on, unripe grapes . . .'

Perry felt someone pushing between him and Carotus.

It was Valentia. She beamed at them both, then turned to Carotus.

'I thought you were doing the picking,' she said.

'They wouldn't let me,' growled Carotus.

'Huh,' said Valentia. She reached for a bunch of grapes and began popping them in her mouth. 'This one's a bit green,' she said, tossing it away.

In a flash, Perry opened his mouth and snapped it out of the air. The other two goggled at him, then the next instant all three of them were throwing grapes to each other, mouths gaping, bobbing and laughing, with grapes showering around them onto the floor.

'Boys, stop that!' snapped the angry voice of toilet woman.

But Valentia just gave her a smirk, and kept on eating the grapes off her own bunch.

How come Valentia doesn't get told off too? wondered Perry.

Then he realised. A slave couldn't scold the daughter of her master.

'That basket needs emptying,' said toilet woman crossly.

One of the men hoisted it to his bare shoulder, carried it up the steps to a platform and tipped the grapes into a large stone trough.

The treading pit! thought Perry.

'Firmo, is it full?' called Valentia.

The man shook his head.

'One more load will do it, though,' he announced, as he brought back the basket.

At that, everyone at the bench broke into a frenzy, grabbing bunches and plucking as fast as they could.

'This basket's nearly full!' called one of the sorters.

'Mine too!' called another woman.

Firmo and another man edged closer . . .

Up on the platform, men were shinning up ladders to hang ropes from beams over the pit.

They're getting ready for the treading, thought Perry.

Suddenly, a roar went up. The other man had leapt ahead of Firmo, grabbed one of the baskets and was racing with it up the steps to the platform.

'That's it, the pit's full enough,' he bellowed as he poured in the grapes, Firmo close behind him.

The next instant, the two men were clambering over the side and catching hold of the ropes.

Valentia threw down the grapes she was holding. 'I'm joining in,' she yelled.

Perry took a step to follow then realised Carotus was hanging back. The slave boy was watching Valentia, his faced filled with envy.

Valentia bounded up the steps, kicking off her shoes as she ran. At the top, she hoisted up her long skirt, bunching it over her belt to leave her lower legs bare. Laughing, she turned, glanced around, then looked down at Perry and Carotus.

'Come on, you two!' she cried. Pelting back

down the stairs, she grabbed them both by the wrists. 'Come on, you help too.'

Carotus was grinning from ear to ear, and Perry knew his own face was split in a wide smile as they ran up the steps.

The men in the pit were stomping around, crushing the grapes with their big bare feet. Quickly, Perry and Carotus yanked off their sandals and the three of them climbed onto the wall of the pit.

'Go!' cried Valentia, and they all jumped off together.

'*Va-ah!*' squealed Valentia, as her feet began to slide.

'Woa-oah!' cried Perry, just managing to keep his balance as she gripped his hand to stop herself falling over.

Carotus was windmilling his arms and laughing.

'Hey!' yelled Firmo.

Valentia stood there, wobbling and laughing too.

'Those boys aren't big enough,' muttered Firmo.

Valentia beamed at him. 'I say they can help,' she said. 'Come on, Carotus. Come on, Peregrinus.'

Firmo must be a slave, thought Perry. *He can't tell Valentia what to do.*

Clinging together, Perry, Valentia and Carotus waded into the centre, grapes squishing and exploding under their bare toes.

'This feels funny,' laughed Perry. The lumps and ridges of seeds and stalks poked into the soles of his feet.

There was a burst of music from the floor below. Perry glanced down. A boy was blowing a strange-looking instrument, and everyone in the room started to sing. It wasn't Latin, though, it seemed to be some other weird language.

'*Geneta uimpi*,' they chanted, '*da mi linda.*'

'What are they singing?' yelled Perry, in Carotus's ear.

'It's the old Gaulish language,' Carotus shouted back.

'It means, "Pretty girl, give me drinks,"' smirked Valentia.

Valentia and Carotus joined in, and after a moment, Perry did too.

This is fun, he thought. *Lucky I didn't think up the right word last night, or I'd be missing out!*

Catching a rope with his free hand, he began to stomp and squelch even harder.

'You're splashing me,' laughed Valentia.

Perry felt a sloshing under his feet. It felt like he was stamping in a wading pool.

'Here comes the must!' bellowed Firmo, and the cry was taken up around the room.

'Here comes the must!' 'Here comes the must!'

Perry found himself being hauled with the others towards the side of the pit.

'*Ecce!* Look!' cried Firmo, smiling broadly and pointing over the edge.

Perry gazed at the pale, rose-tinted juice that Firmo called 'must' trickling out the holes in the stone wall of the pit.

'We helped make that!' cried Valentia.

Wait till I tell Mum about this! thought Perry.

12

BOXERS

'I'VE NEVER TRIED THESE BEFORE,' said Perry, dipping his hand warily in the basket of purple figs.

It was lunchtime, and he and Carotus were squatting with Firmo and the other workers around a picnic spread out on the cobblestones of the yard.

'Do you eat the peel?' asked Perry, pulling out a fruit and turning it in his fingers. It had furry skin, like a peach.

He glanced up. Carotus was gaping at him, his hands, holding a fig, suspended in mid-air.

'What do you mean, you've never eaten one before?' demanded Carotus. 'Everyone eats figs!'

'I . . .' Perry stared back in confusion. 'Er . . . just kidding,' he mumbled.

Carotus gave him an odd look, then tore his fig in half.

Perry hesitated, then did the same. The fruit was smaller than a peach and there was no stone in the centre. It looked a bit like a strawberry inside. He took a cautious bite.

Yum! It was as sweet as a grape.

Beside him, Firmo gave a noisy belch. 'Drink and live,' he grunted, swigging from a large pottery mug.

Licking his fingers, Carotus picked up the jug in front of him, and sloshed some sort of pale, murky mixture into two more mugs.

'Drink and live!' he responded

Perry picked up the other mug. It smelt disgusting, but he was so thirsty . . . He tried a tiny sip. *Eurrgh!* It tasted like vinegar and milk, but when he looked around for somewhere to spit it, he saw Gabrina bearing down on them. He sprang to his feet, swallowing the horrible mouthful.

'What have you two been up to?' boomed the housekeeper. 'You look as if you've fallen in a vat of wine!'

Perry glanced at his pink-streaked legs, and his tunic, dripping with grape juice.

Carotus grinned up at her. 'We helped with the treading,' he said.

'That's not your job,' snapped Gabrina. 'Get

yourselves to the bathhouse. *Now!*' she added, when Carotus picked up a hunk of bread.

'Old cow-face,' growled Carotus as she bustled away. He dunked his bread in a bowl of stinky garum, and rose slowly, stuffing it in his mouth. 'Come on,' he said.

They passed the kitchen and the awful toilet.

'The slave bathhouse is next to the latrine,' said Carotus, waving his hand, 'but I just have to fetch a change of tunic and ... Hang on, where are your spare clothes? I forgot to ask you last night.'

'I ...' Perry thought wildly. 'I lost them.'

Carotus glanced around, then leaned forward excitedly. 'You've run away from somewhere, haven't you?' he whispered. 'I know, because I saw you when the master arrived – remember?' He straightened up, grinning broadly. 'You were on *this* side of the gate. So you couldn't have come with him.'

Perry opened his mouth.

'Don't worry, I won't give you away,' chortled Carotus, and he darted off without waiting for an answer.

Outside the two-storey bakery, the big black guard dogs were stretched on the cobblestones, lazing in the sunshine. They barely lifted their noses when the boys walked past and entered the front door.

Crossing the room to the bedchamber, Carotus eyed Perry up and down. 'You're nearly my size,' he said. 'I'll lend you a tunic till someone weaves you a new one.'

I'm not going to stay here that long! thought Perry.

Carotus dragged a green tunic, and then a brown one, out of the wooden clothes chest and bundled them into Perry's arms.

'And here, you can carry the towels too,' he said, piling them on top.

'Hey, I'm not your slave,' Perry started to protest, then stopped.

That wasn't a joke here ... people really *were* slaves!

He rested his chin on the folded towels. They were linen, like the tea towels at home. *But not as clean and white,* thought Perry.

'And I'll bring this,' said Carotus.

With a loud jangle, he pulled a bunch of weird bronze objects out of the chest. They hung from a large ring, and Perry stared at them, swinging and clashing together as he followed Carotus to the bathhouse.

As they passed the arbour and the courtyard garden, Carotus waved his arm.

'That's where I usually work,' he said. 'When I'm not serving meals. I expect you will too. Now, here's the bathhouse.'

They stepped into a small, dark, stuffy room that had nothing in it except a bare wooden bench. Perry looked around. There was no bath. There was not even a jug and basin like they'd used at dinner.

'How do we wash?' he asked, then immediately wished he hadn't. Carotus was staring at him again.

'What do you mean, *how do we wash*?' Carotus demanded. 'You must come from a very strange place! In the bath, of course! It's through there.' He pointed at a slightly open door across the room. Then, '*Eia*, where are you going?' he called, as Perry headed for the door. 'You've got to get undressed first!'

Perry peeked at the bath – it was big and square, like a spa bath – and turned back.

Carotus was just dropping his tunic on the floor. Underneath, he had nothing on at all. But instead of heading for the bath, he sat on the bench, unhooked a ball-shaped bronze bottle from his ring, and yanked out the bronze stopper.

Perry stared as he poured something that looked like olive oil on the palm of his hand and began to rub it all over himself. Then he did something even stranger. Using a curved blade – like one of the grape-cutting knives, only thicker and blunter – he began to scrape it all off again.

'Come on,' he called, glancing up, 'what are you waiting for?'

'Uh . . .'

Slowly, Perry placed his stylus on the floor, untied his belt and pulled his tunic over his head. It was only when he heard Carotus let out a shriek that he remembered the silky blue boxer shorts he was wearing underneath.

'What the Jupiter are you wearing?' gasped Carotus.

Suddenly, Perry had had enough of pretending to be a slave.

'*Boxers*,' he declared.

'Boxus?' echoed Carotus blankly.

Perry laughed. 'Not boxus. *Boxers. Boxer shorts.* And you're right. I *do* come from somewhere strange.' He locked his eyes onto Carotus's face as he blurted out the truth. 'I come from . . . the future!'

He waited for a reaction.

But, to his disappointment, his new friend only snorted.

'Ha! Keep your secrets if you want to,' scoffed Carotus. 'You can't fool me with a story like that! Now, come on . . .' He held out the bronze tools. 'It's your turn with the oil and the strigil.'

13

THE HOLE
IN THE STONE

COVERED IN OLIVE OIL NOW, as well as grape juice, Perry stepped awkwardly into the water and sat down. It was embarrassing, sharing a bath with a boy he hardly knew.

'It's hot!' he exclaimed in surprise.

Carotus rolled his eyes. 'I can't believe you never had a hot bath before. You really did come from a strange place.' He leaned back and closed his eyes. 'The water's heated by a fire,' he said. 'It's the kitchen furnace, behind the wall.'

'Oh.' Perry looked around. 'Where's . . .' he started to ask, and then stopped. Maybe the Romans didn't use soap in their baths.

He was still trying to work out how to get clean, when Carotus scrambled out again.

'Come on, lazy,' he called, 'we've got work to do. There are guests coming for dinner.'

At least, thought Perry, wrapping himself in his scrap of towel, *I know all about dinners now.*

But he was wrong.

While the guests were taking their places on the dining couch, Gabrina thrust a water jug and basin into Perry's hands.

'Do you know what to do?' she growled.

'Yes,' said Perry with relief. He'd seen Rittia doing this yesterday.

He took a step towards the nearest guest and held out the jug and basin. The man looked at him.

Perry poured a little water in the basin and waited expectantly.

The man waited too, a scowl beginning to crease his face.

In a flash of movement, Carotus leapt to Perry's side.

'Wash his feet!' hissed Carotus in a low voice.

'Wha-at?' Perry looked around, confused.

The next moment, Carotus was kneeling down and pulling off the man's shoes.

Hours later, as they were heading back to their bedchamber, Perry was still fuming at the memory of having to wash all those disgusting, stinky feet.

The instant he was through the door, he dropped onto his sleeping mat and yanked the stylus out of his belt.

TAKE ME HOME! he scrawled, digging the tip deep into the earth floor.

But, to his annoyance, when he looked up, Carotus was still there. The slave boy was sitting on his own bed, staring. 'What are you doing?' he demanded.

'Trying to get back to my own time,' growled Perry. 'This stylus brought me here, so . . .'

'Oh no.' Carotus rolled his eyes. 'Are you still pretending you come from the future?'

'I do!' insisted Perry. 'And when I find the right word, you'll see, I will disappear right in front of you. Watch.'

'*Vah.*' Carotus rolled over to sleep, but Perry stayed on his knees, scribbling away in the dark, quiet room. It was only when he heard Poppillus coming in from the bakery that he pushed the stylus under his mat and lay down.

In the morning, he promised himself.

In the morning, though, there was no time.

'Get up,' cried Carotus, shaking him awake. 'There's something weird happening.'

Perry opened one eye. The room was still dark. 'It's not morning yet,' he complained.

'Yes it is, it's dawn. The cocks are crowing, the geese are honking, the calves are crying ... And there's someone shouting in the workyard. Come on. Let's see what's going on.'

Perry stumbled to his feet, pushing the hair out of his eyes.

The guard dogs were barking as Perry and Carotus raced past them. The sky was just growing light but from the other side of the workyard wall came the sound of chanting, and then loud shouts, and scraping and banging noises.

'What the Jupiter?' exploded Carotus.

The boys burst into the yard, then skidded to a halt, and stared.

The double doors of the building opposite were flung open, and a group of men and boys were staggering out, hauling a huge block of stone.

'One ... two ... heave!' they chanted. 'One ... two ... he-e-eave!'

They staggered a few steps, crashed the stone down, and stood panting. Then they braced themselves to lift it again.

'It's the weight stone!' Carotus exclaimed. 'From the olive press.' He turned to the slaves idling outside the kitchen. 'What are they doing?' he demanded.

Tiluvimpus sniffed and blew his nose on his fingers. 'See that Dannorix,' he said, jerking his chin at a man directing the stone-moving. 'The one who thinks he's a gift from the gods because the master brought him from up north – no offence, young fella,' he added, looking at Perry. 'Well, seems the master saw some fancy new style of press up north, and that Dannorix is supposed to be getting them to make it here. They've got to change the weight stone or something.' He sniffed again.

They all watched as the stone reached the middle of the yard and Dannorix told the men to stop.

'Which of you is Oxittus, the stonemason?' he called.

A wiry man wearing nothing but a sleeve-less tunic strolled forward. The muscles in his arms and legs looked as hard and sinewy as if he had carved them.

'I'm Oxittus,' he said.

'Well, Oxittus . . .'

The other men headed towards the kitchen, shouting for drinks, but Dannorix and Oxittus knelt down beside the stone. Dannorix began pointing at it, marking out a circle in the centre, banging his hands as if hammering a hole, and then pointing out other marks . . .

Perry felt a ripple of shock as memory washed

over him. A weight stone with a hole in the middle . . . Could this be the actual stone he'd seen at the château – the one with the extra hole made by mistake?

He spun round to Carotus. 'I know what they're doing,' he cried.

'Everyone can see what they're doing,' scoffed Carotus. 'They're making a hole.'

'No, I mean . . . I know what's going to *happen*,' cried Perry. 'And I can prove to you I come from the future. That man . . .' he flung out his arm, '. . . is going to make a mistake. He's going to carve an extra hole in the wrong place!'

Carotus burst out laughing. 'You and your stories!' he guffawed.

Perry crossed his arms. 'You wait and see!' he said. 'I'll be right, and then you'll believe I'm from the future.'

14

WINE

PERRY'S LAST WORDS WERE DROWNED out by shouts as a crowd of men came tramping through the far gate with a tree trunk balanced on their shoulders. Dannorix jumped to his feet.

'*Vah*, what's going on now?!' cried Carotus.

The new arrivals dumped their load beside the stone, then two of them stepped forward with handfuls of tools.

'The carpenters from up north,' said Carotus. 'They must be making something for the press.'

But Perry was only interested in the stone. He kept his eyes on Oxittus, just glancing every now and then at the carpenters.

The sun rose, and in the heat and bustle, no one paid attention to the watching boys. Dannorix grew red in the face. The strands of dark hair he wore combed over his bald patch flapped from the side of his head like a flag. The carpenters, looking hot in their long, heavy tunics, began to mark out a spiral shape at one end of the tree trunk.

'What's that supposed to be?' wondered Carotus.

'Looks like a screw,' said Perry. 'The biggest screw in the world!'

Then his own words from the future came back to him. He remembered kneeling on the floor in the château, reading the label on the weight stone, and saying, 'What on earth's a winch press . . . or a screw press?'

Of course! This was going to be the screw press!

And now he was absolutely certain this was the stone he had seen in the château, the one with the mistake.

As he spun back to Oxittus, he felt Carotus nudging his shoulder.

'So, where's this mistake?' jeered Carotus in his ear.

'It'll happen. You'll see.'

'Sure. And last night you promised you were going to disappear, and you didn't,' scoffed Carotus.

Perry chuckled, and patted his stylus. 'I'm going to stay now till Oxittus makes his mistake,' he said.

'I want to see your face when you find out I'm really from the future. But then, I'll disappear.'

'Ha.'

For the rest of that day, and all through the next, Perry kept breaking off in the middle of chores, to rush to the workyard and check what was happening.

Slowly, the whole trunk of wood took on the shape of a giant screw.

Slowly, very slowly, Oxittus worked on the stone. The stonemason finished the big hole in the middle, but then, to Perry's frustration, he disappeared. The weight stone was left, lying alone, in the middle of the yard.

'Where's Oxittus gone?' Perry demanded of the carpenters.

'Making the iron brackets,' grunted one of them, hammering away with his chisel. 'He's a black-smith too.'

When Perry and Carotus reached the workyard on the third morning, it was full of people hurrying over the cobblestones with large jugs in their hands.

'They're moving the first must,' said Carotus excitedly, 'that juice from the grapes we helped to tread. They're taking it to the wine cellar.'

And then, between the slaves heading for the building at the back of the yard, Perry noticed a lone figure kneeling by the weight stone.

'Oxittus is back!' he cried.

He shot across the cobblestones, dodged around all the people with their brimming jugs, and reached the stonemason's side.

Oxittus had an iron bracket in his hand. He placed it on the stone, moved it across a bit, nodded, then picked up a sharp, pointed tool.

Perry's breath caught in his throat. He flung around as Carotus came running up beside him.

'This is it,' whispered Perry excitedly. 'This is when he makes a mistake! Watch!'

The stonemason pressed the sharp point through a hole in the bracket and made a mark in the stone. At that moment, the voice of Gabrina rang out across the courtyard.

'Carotus, Peregrinus, stop dawdling.'

Perry looked at Carotus in dismay as she marched across the yard, heading for the wine cellar.

'Go on, I need some garlands,' she ordered. 'Be off with you! Hurry!'

Fuming, Perry rose to his feet.

'Why does she need garlands at this time of day?' he grumbled as he followed Carotus to the garden.

'For making an offering to the wine god.'

Carotus sang as he wove the ivy into a chain, and Perry knelt beside him, impatiently tearing off flowers and handing them to him. The sun beat down on them, the air brimmed with scents from the garden, the cicadas droned, and the sound of voices drifted from the workyard.

'Come on,' urged Perry.

At last, Carotus was finished.

'Here, you carry this one,' he said.

To Perry's surprise, the wine cellar was not underground like the one at the château. As they followed Gabrina inside, he saw a long room with rounded tops of clay jars showing through holes in the floor. Two men were crouched over an open jar, filling it from jugs in their hands.

'Those wine jars under the ground are so big, you can stand in them,' whispered Carotus. 'I climbed inside one once, when they were cleaning it.'

It'll take lots of jugs to fill them then! thought Perry.

A shrine stood just by the door. It had a single statue on it – a little bronze god wearing a crown of grapes and leaves.

The housekeeper held out her hand for the garlands. 'Now, go,' she ordered. 'You have plenty of work to do.'

As they stepped outside, Carotus grabbed Perry by the sleeve. 'Quick, come and look in the wine-pressing room!' he said.

'But I want to ...' Perry glanced anxiously towards the stone.

'They can't have done much yet. Come on, quick, while Gabrina's not looking.'

The pressing room was a hubbub of noise and people. Workers swarmed over the vats, the sorting benches, the treading pit, the platform . . .

'Come and see how the must looks now,' yelled Carotus, dragging Perry towards one of the vats.

A mob of men and boys were clustered around the vat, laughing and holding out empty jugs. While inside the vat . . . Perry stared in amazement. The fermenting juice was bubbling and foaming, and two slaves, naked except for cloths around their hips, were wading in it, scooping up bucketfuls and pouring them into the jugs being thrust towards them.

The colour had faded from rose pink to palest gold so it looked as if they were plunging around in a vat of champagne. A heady scent filled the air, smelling like wine already.

'Carotus,' bellowed Salutus, the head winemaker. 'What are you and that new boy doing in here? Scram.'

'All right,' called Carotus. But, 'Look over here first,' he said, pulling Perry through the crowd again.

A massive beam dangled by ropes from the ceiling rafters, and two men had just lowered it to rest on a tower of baskets.

'That's the wine press,' said Carotus. 'It would kill someone if it fell on them,' he added with relish.

'What's in the baskets?' asked Perry.

'Squashed grapeskins from the treading pit,' said Carotus. 'Firmo's going to crush them more. Watch!'

Firmo was waiting below the platform. Beside him, a rope hung from the end of the beam down to a wooden winch on a frame. And the frame . . .

Perry let out a gasp. The frame was joined to a huge, heavy block of stone.

Noooo! Not *another* weight stone! This place was crawling with them. What if the one in the yard wasn't the right one?

Firmo took hold of a rod jutting out of the winch, and hauled the rod towards him. Beads of sweat broke out on his forehead and his arms shook with the strain. With a loud *creak*, the rope began to wind, and the beam inched downwards.

'See!' Carotus pointed excitedly as liquid streamed through the baskets.

But Perry knelt down, trying to look at the stone.

'Does this stone have holes in it?' he asked.

Carotus shook his head. 'Not yet. But they're going to change the wine press to the new style too, when they finish the grape harvest.'

Perry looked at him in dismay. 'How long will that take?' he asked.

Carotus shrugged. 'Thirty days? Forty days?'

Forty days! Perry didn't want to hang around here for forty days! He'd wanted to prove to Carotus that he came from the future, but not if it meant he'd have to stay here for another forty days!

'Carotus!' bellowed Salutus again. 'I told you boys to scram.'

As he hurried out to the workyard, Perry threw a hopeful glance towards Oxittus.

And his heart leapt with excitement.

There, in the middle of the yard, stood Dannorix, yelling and shaking his fist while poor Oxittus sat in a dejected heap, and slaves stood around with jugs in their hands, gawping.

'Why didn't you check with me before you started drilling?' shouted Dannorix. 'Now you've put a hole in the wrong place!'

Perry felt as if his whole body was breaking into a smile. He turned triumphantly to Carotus.

'See, what did I tell you?' he declared.

Carotus stared back at him, too astonished to speak.

'And now,' said Perry, reaching for his stylus, 'I can go home.'

15

THE WAX TABLET

PERRY PEEKED AROUND THE DOOR of the small room that was used for lessons. Grumpy Gabrina had told him to join the classes this morning, but the others hadn't arrived yet. He hesitated, then slipped inside.

Any other time, he would have reached for his stylus and grabbed the chance to scratch a few words, but now . . . He heaved a sigh. He'd been stuck here for two weeks. Nothing he wrote seemed to work. He'd have to find a different way home.

He looked around. Every time he saw a new room, he imagined how he'd describe it to his family: a high-backed chair woven from cane, like a basket; stools padded with striped cushions; walls painted with red and black panels at the top, and purplish squiggles to look like marble at the bottom; the window, just a square hole with wooden shutters; the floor . . .

The *floor*!

'That's the mosaic I saw in the ruin!' he gasped out loud.

There was the border of twisting snakes, and the flower he'd found under the tarpaulin. He gazed around with awe. It was strange seeing it all so perfect and clean. He remembered kneeling on those tiles when they were broken and dirty, stroking them with his fingers . . .

He stared down at his hands, then at the floor again. If it wasn't the stylus that had taken him back in time, maybe it was this floor!

He threw himself on his knees and pressed his hands eagerly on the tiny stone squares.

'*Please*,' he whispered, 'take me back to my own time.' He pictured the relief and joy in his family's faces when he turned up again; he could almost feel Dad's arms, hugging him close. '*Ple-e-ease*,' he repeated.

He squeezed his eyes shut, waited, then opened them again.

The basket chair was still in front of him, and the stools, and the funny painted walls.

He sagged in disappointment.

From outside came the sound of voices, and he sprang to his feet.

Through the wide-open door, he looked out on a patch of courtyard. He could see water trickling from the mouth of the dolphin fountain and a small, leafy tree in a pot.

A citron, he thought, remembering what Carotus had called it. The tree had strange, bright yellow fruit like huge, lumpy lemons.

And here came Carotus, swinging a clay jug with holes in the side, using it like a watering can. Balbus, the tutor, waddled beside him. As usual, Balbus was reciting one of his favourite quotes.

'*Guard that which is entrusted to thy care,*' he intoned.

The portly old man reached the doorway and turned in, peering short-sightedly around. 'Where is Valentia?' he quavered.

Perry shrugged. 'Not here yet,' he said. 'But I'm a new pupil.'

'Ah, *the kind master favours his slave with the gift of education,*' observed the old man.

Perry watched as he set a pile of strange-looking objects on a side table. They were rectangles of wood, bound together in pairs by leather loops along one edge.

What are they? wondered Perry. *They look like wooden laptops!*

Balbus collapsed on the basket chair, leaned his head back, and raised one foot.

'Footstool,' he wheezed.

His legs, below his knee-length green tunic, were wrapped in strips of grey cloth, and lumpy nailheads stuck out all over the soles of his leather sandals.

Perry shoved a low stool under his feet.

Carotus came in next. 'Where's Valentia?' he said.

At that moment, they all heard running footsteps, and her voice calling excitedly. 'Come on, hurry up, Quintio.'

She burst into the room, her hair loose and messy around her face, her cheeks flushed.

'Look what I've brought,' she cried.

She swept out her arm and a boy in a dirty tunic came stumbling in after her carrying a large, lidded basket.

'Put it down in the middle of the floor,' ordered Valentia. Then she beamed at the others. 'You'll never guess,' she said. 'Cat's had kittens! I told Quintio to bring them here. Open the lid, Quintio.'

But before the farm slave could obey, a woman appeared in the doorway, puffing and looking worried.

'Valentia!' she gasped. 'Where've you been?' It was Habita, Valentia's nursemaid.

'Just to the barns,' said Valentia, smiling sweetly. 'And I found kittens! Go on, show them, Quintio.'

As the slave reached down to flip back the lid, Perry noticed red scratches all over his bare arms. The cat's head reared out of the basket, hissing angrily, and Quintio leapt out of the way.

'Sssh, Cat,' soothed Valentia. She crouched to look, but didn't move any closer. 'Look at the kittens. Aren't they *cute*? And Father says I can choose one for a pet when it's old enough!'

From a safe distance, Perry eyed the tiny, curled-up balls of fluff. Most of them were striped brown and white, like the mother, but one of them was bright ginger.

'Children, children, it is lesson time,' called the tutor peevishly. 'Remember, *an ignorant life is like death*!'

Neither Valentia nor Carotus paid him any attention.

'Valentia …' reproached Habita, putting her hands on her hips.

To Perry's surprise, the girl rose to her feet. It seemed the nursemaid was the one slave who could tell her what to do.

Valentia took a wooden folder from the side table and perched on a stool. Perry copied her and she flashed him a smile. For the first time, he noticed the dimple in her cheek.

'Come on, son, you too,' prompted Habita.

Grinning broadly, Carotus dragged a stool along the floor, making a loud scraping noise.

Habita shook her head at him, but, 'They're ready for you now, Balbus,' she said, and left the room.

The old man heaved a sigh. 'We begin with dictation,' he bleated.

But Valentia was already looking away from him. 'Oh no, what's she doing?' she cried, pointing at the cat basket. The mother cat was climbing out, a kitten held by the scruff of its neck between her teeth.

The cat began heading towards the door.

'She's eating it!' wailed Valentia. 'Quintio, save it!'

But Quintio had slipped out of the room.

'It's all right,' Perry reassured her. 'That's how cats carry their kittens. She's probably trying to take it back to the barn.'

'Oh.'

They all watched the cat head out the door.

'Children, children,' wailed Balbus. 'Write down this quote from . . .'

'I don't have a stylus,' said Valentia.

'Me neither,' said Carotus.

They jumped up and began wandering around, looking on all the side tables, and giggling. Valentia opened a cupboard. Perry caught a glimpse of scrolls inside, then she reached onto a shelf. 'I found one.'

'I've got mine,' said Perry, pulling it out of his belt.

'Carotus, you use mine,' said the tutor testily. 'Now all of you, sit down!'

Perry opened his folder. The wood inside was coated with . . . *Wax!* thought Perry excitedly. *That's the proper thing to use a stylus on! Maybe that's what I need to make it work.*

The board wobbled wildly on his lap as he scrawled every word he could think of: FUTURE, ELECTRICITY, HOME . . .

But when he looked up, Balbus was still there.

'Today,' quavered the tutor, 'you will inscribe these wise words from Cato: *Strive after noble deeds.*'

Valentia smoothed the wax first by rubbing it with the stubby end of her stylus. As Perry hastily did the same, she leaned towards him. 'Don't bother writing what he tells us,' she confided. 'He's so old and blind he can't read anymore. I'm just writing my name.'

She pressed the tip of her stylus into the wax and, to Perry's surprise, she drew a large letter C.

'Your name doesn't start with C,' he whispered.

'You don't need to whisper. Balbus can't hear properly either,' said Valentia. 'And anyway, my name does start with C. My full name is Camilla Valentia.'

'But . . .' Perry's words came out in a squeak. 'That can't be your name!'

She looked at him, chuckling. 'You say such funny things. Why can't it be?'

'Because . . .'

He couldn't tell her it was because he'd seen the coffin of a girl called Camilla Valentia at the museum in Arles.

He watched in horror as she finished writing her name and handed her board to Balbus.

'There you are!' she declared, and she arched her eyebrows at her friends as the old man nodded, peering at it short-sightedly.

'You two are so slow,' said Valentia, smirking.

Perry's eyes followed her as she knelt down beside the cat basket. When her hair flopped forward, he thought how soft it looked, as soft as kittens' fur.

'Look, I've drawn a cat,' said Carotus, holding out his wax tablet to Perry. 'What do you think?'

'I . . . I think it's good,' said Perry, but he wasn't really looking.

He was still watching Valentia. She couldn't be the girl who died. She couldn't be!

Carotus leaned close, dropping his voice so Valentia couldn't hear. 'Do you have wax tablets and styluses in the future?' he whispered.

'Uh . . .' Perry tried to focus on him. 'We have . . . tablets,' he said, 'but we write on them by touching them with our fingers.'

Carotus looked at him in delight, then straightened up hastily as Valentia came back to her seat, sucking the back of her hand.

'Those kittens have sharp claws,' she complained. 'What are you two whispering about?'

'Uh . . .'

'Boys, have you finished your dictation?' asked the old tutor.

Grinning, Carotus handed over his cat picture.

Perry looked down at the waxed piece of wood lying on his lap, but all he could see were the words 'Camilla Valentia' engraved on the stone coffin. And the age: eleven years, two months and one day. He remembered Valentia, in the dining room, saying she was nearly eleven . . .

He wished he'd never been to Arles. He wished he'd never seen—

Wait a minute. In *Arles*?!

Of course! The girl in the coffin had come from Arles, and this Camilla Valentia lived nearly two hundred kilometres away, here at the villa. He grinned in relief.

The girl from the coffin couldn't be this Camilla Valentia.

I was just being silly, he thought.

16

BUCCO

'I'VE MISSED ALL THE FOOTY, I've missed the Grand Final, and I don't even have a proper ball to play with,' growled Perry, stabbing his stylus over and over into the dirt. 'I'm sick of being a stupid slave. I'm sick of washing other people's feet. I'm sick of making boring flower garlands. And I'm sick of eating figs with every single meal. Every single day!'

He hurled the stylus down and slumped back on his heels.

I've been stuck here for six weeks now, he thought miserably. *If I ever get out, I bet my family won't even be in France anymore. They'll think I'm dead. They'll . . .*

'France!' he yelled out loud, snatching up his stylus again.

That's what I'm doing wrong! he thought. *In the future, they'll talk French here – I should be writing in French!*

Slashing his stylus through the earth, he wrote the only two French words he knew – BONJOUR and ZUT – and looked up expectantly.

'Pff,' he snorted in frustration.

'*Eia*, Peregrinus, *ei* . . . Where's Carotus?'

Perry thrust his stylus in his belt and jumped to his feet. Valentia had appeared in the courtyard and was looking around.

Perry looked around too. 'Don't know,' he answered.

Carotus had told him where he was going, but Perry hadn't been listening. He was too busy writing.

'I'm choosing my kitten now,' said Valentia, 'and I wanted him to help.' She put her hands on her hips and looked around crossly, as if she expected Carotus to be always sitting there, waiting to do her bidding. Then her eyes came back to Perry. 'You seemed to know about kittens the other day,' she said.

'A bit.' Some of his friends had cats.

'Good.' Valentia's face broke into a smile. 'You help me, then. Here, carry this.'

She held out a tiny clay jar.

Perry looked at it and nearly burst out laughing.

Do you really need a slave to carry that? he wanted to ask. Shrugging, he took it out of her hand.

The kittens lived with the mother cat in a sprawling stone barn. As Perry and Valentia hurried towards it, they passed the big bathhouse where the master and his family washed, and then workers in the fig orchard, filling up baskets with purple-streaked fruit. *More figs!* sighed Perry.

They slipped through the door of the barn, and he gazed around in awe. Everywhere he looked there were stores of food: huge clay jars of lentils, bulging sacks of peas and beans, barrels of dried figs — not more figs! — and all sorts of grains piled into heaps.

'Kittens, look what I've brought you,' called Valentia, and, taking the jar back, she pulled off the lid and set it on the floor.

The smell of stinky fish sauce wafted into the air, and two brown kittens came leaping into view around a barrel of figs.

'Here,' cried Valentia kneeling down and poking her finger in the garum. 'It's yummy fish,' she called.

The kittens padded over and sniffed her finger with their little pink noses. Then they scampered off, their tiny soft paws making no sound at all on the barn floor.

'You silly things,' said Valentia.

But now there was a scrabbling noise behind them, and Perry and Valentia spun round. The orange kitten was perched at the very top of a heap of barley grains. He stared at them, his oversized, pointy ears sticking straight up, his green eyes wide. Then he tumbled and slid down the mountain of grain, somersaulted to the floor, and came sprinting towards them.

'Good boy,' said Valentia, offering her finger again.

This time, a little tongue shot out for a taste, before the tiny cat thrust his face right into the jar, and didn't stop gobbling till he'd knocked over the jar and finished off every scrap. Then he looked up at her, miaowing hopefully, and licking his lips.

'You're just like Bucco!' chuckled Valentia, picking him up. 'Do you know who Bucco is?' she asked Perry.

He shook his head.

'He's a character in a show. Mother took me to the theatre in town once. It was such fun, all those people clowning around on the stage, and the funniest . . .' She started to giggle. '. . . was Bucco! You should have seen him. He had this puffy-cheeked mask and he pretended to stuff food in it!'

Still laughing, she buried her face in the little cat's soft downy back.

'I pick you for my pet,' she murmured. 'Let's take you to show Carotus.'

As they made their way down the steps from the barn, she pointed at an orchard of silvery trees growing on the hill in the distance.

'Father's dying for those olives to be ready for picking,' she said. 'He can't wait to try out his new press.'

Carotus was standing in the middle of the courtyard, and he thrust something behind his back when they appeared.

'Listen to this,' he called.

'Look at my kitten,' Valentia cried at the same time.

She ran over to him, holding out the cat, but Carotus didn't even glance at her hands. He had a huge, mischievous grin spread over his face.

'Listen,' he said again.

The next minute, a very rude noise sounded from behind his back.

'Carotus!' shrieked Valentia.

Perry tried not to laugh.

Then Carotus brought his arms from around his back to reveal something that looked like a floppy pink balloon in his hands.

'They were killing a pig and I got the bladder,' he said triumphantly. 'I'm going to do this at dinner tonight behind Gabrina. It's going to be the best joke ever! Listen, I'll do it again.'

He held the bladder to his lips and began to blow. As it grew into a round balloon shape, Perry almost exploded with excitement.

'Here, we can play ball with that!' he cried. 'Tie up the end and give it to me.'

He reached for the bladder but Carotus swung it away. 'No,' he protested. 'If I tie it up, I won't be able to make noises with it anymore.'

'Go on!' pleaded Perry. He hadn't been able to play ball for six weeks.

'Oh, all right,' said Carotus, then laughed as he let the air out again with another noisy *ffft* before passing it over.

'And now, look at my kitten,' burst out Valentia, thrusting him under Carotus's nose. 'He's called Bucco.'

'He's got hair like mine,' said Carotus. 'Let's see what he thinks of the garden.'

As Carotus placed the kitten on the path, Perry puffed eagerly at the bladder. It was slimy, and not as heavy as a real football. *But it's better than nothing!* he thought.

'Here,' he called. The others had chased the kitten round the other side of the courtyard. For a moment Perry paused, relishing the familiar feel of a ball in his hands, then, 'Get ready to catch,' he yelled.

He gave the bladder the biggest kick he could. There was a satisfying *whoomp*, and it sailed right over the pond.

'Get it!' he cried.

But Carotus and Valentia just stood there watching as it sailed towards them and landed with a *thud* on the ground.

'You didn't catch it,' he complained.

'What did you just do?' demanded Carotus.

Perry stared at him. 'I kicked the ball,' he said. 'Don't you . . .?' And then he stopped. Obviously not. 'Hey, don't let the kitten get it,' he yelled as Bucco stretched out his little claws.

Carotus grabbed the ball and backed away.

'This is how we play ball,' he said.

He stood right in front of Valentia and tossed it into her hands. But instead of catching it, she smacked it towards the ground.

'That's boring!' she cried. 'I want to play like Peregrinus.'

Hiking up her long skirt, she tucked it into her sash, and gave the ball a hard thump with her toe. It spun down the path, then stopped.

'Huh,' she grunted. 'How do you get it to fly?'

Perry grinned. 'I'll show you.' He loped forward

and picked it up. 'Like this,' he said, kicking it again. 'Now you try.'

But Carotus reached the ball first. 'Watch me,' he yelled, swinging his leg.

'Straight and steady!' warned Perry, but he was too late.

It bounced off the side of Carotus's foot and trickled into the pond.

As Carotus stood there laughing, Valentia splashed in after it and waded out again, her long skirt trailing. She held it in front of her. 'Ready?'

There was a *SPLAT* from her dripping dress and shoe, and the ball sailed over the stone dolphin in the middle of the pond. Perry ran back, holding out his arms to catch it. He could see it, pink and glistening in the sunlight, and then it thudded against his chest and he wrapped it in his arms.

'Good kick!' he shouted.

But at that instant, Habita, the nursemaid, stepped out of the villa. She stared at them all in astonishment.

'What is going on?' she asked. 'Valentia, what's happened to you?'

Perry looked at Valentia and grinned. She didn't look much like a master's daughter anymore. She was standing there, panting, her cheeks pink, her hair fallen out of her bun, and her dress soaked.

'We're playing kick-ball,' beamed Valentia.

'Well, you're not playing anymore,' said Habita. 'Your mother says you're to go up to the weaving room.'

'I don't want to,' grumbled Valentia. 'My weaving's so crooked, no one can use it anyway. Not even for farm slaves' tunics.'

'That's exactly why you need to practise,' said Habita. 'A lady should know how to weave. Now come on, I'll get you into dry clothes before you go upstairs.'

As Valentia turned for her bedroom, Bucco came loping down the path.

'Bucco!' she cried. 'I nearly forgot about you. This is my new pet,' she said, showing him to her nursemaid.

'You can't take a cat into a weaving room,' said Habita worriedly.

Valentia burst out laughing. 'Bucco will love playing with the wool!' she retorted.

And as the boys went back to their ball, Valentia strutted towards her bedroom, the cat held firmly in her arms.

XVII

17

NEWS

'WATCH WHERE YOU'RE KICKING!' CRIED Perry, but it was too late.

The ball flew off Carotus's foot and crashed onto a rose bush. It deflated with a sad little *whoosh*.

'Oh no!'

They both stared at the flat pink pancake hanging off the branch, then Carotus pulled it off and stretched it in his fingers. There was a big hole in it.

'We can't blow that up again,' sighed Perry.

But Carotus was grinning. He plucked his knife from his belt, slit the hole even wider, and held the bladder over his nose and lips. It was pink, shiny and rubbery, and patterned with spidery red veins. 'How do I look?' he asked.

'Disgusting,' said Perry.

At that moment, a rattle of carriage wheels sounded on the road outside. The boys looked at each other. Who could be headed for the villa at this hour? Visitors to the master usually came in the morning.

As they raced for the front gate, Perry heard footsteps behind them. Dannorix was coming too.

The guard dogs pulled on their chains, barking, and above the bakehouse Perry saw Lollius, Gabrina's grandson, peer from an upstairs window, then turn to run down the stairs.

Carotus dragged open the front gate and a small carriage rattled in over the cobblestones. It was drawn by three mules and Lollius darted forward to take their bridles.

They all watched curiously as a stranger jumped from the carriage. He wore a hooded cape that covered him from neck to knee – *Like those plastic rain ponchos people wear at the footy*, thought Perry – and he had a tall wooden box, shaped like a drum, swinging by a leather strap from his fist.

'I carry a letter from the Emperor Constantine,' he announced.

'From the emperor!' squeaked Lollius, and Carotus looked as if his eyes were about to pop out of his head.

Slowly and ceremoniously, the messenger unlocked the box, and drew out a yellowy-coloured scroll, bound with cords and a fancy-looking seal. He lifted it to read the swirling letters written on the outside in black ink.

'To Rubius Valentius Maximus,' he read aloud, 'at Villa Rubia in the territory of Forum Julii.' He lowered the scroll. 'Is this Villa Rubia?' he enquired.

'Yes, yes!' exclaimed little Lollius, jigging up and down.

'This is indeed Villa Rubia,' Dannorix replied. 'If you follow this boy to the office . . .' he gestured at Carotus, 'I will inform the master of your arrival. Lollius, lead the mules to the stables, where someone can tend to them.'

The office was at the front of the villa. When Carotus came out the door again, Perry pounced on him. 'What's it all about?' he demanded.

'I don't know,' said Carotus. 'He wouldn't tell me. But it must be something important. I— Quick, here comes the master!' He snapped open his knife and trimmed a few straggly twigs from a citron tree. 'Look busy,' he urged.

Perry snatched up the watering jug just as Maximus and Dannorix appeared. The master's hair hung in damp dark curls on his forehead. *He must have jumped out of his bath*, thought Perry. *I've never seen him so excited.*

Maximus almost ran into the front room, Dannorix at his heels. There was a murmur of voices, and Perry and Carotus edged towards the open door, straining to hear what they were saying. But just as they reached it, Maximus burst out of the office and the two boys jumped back, gaping, as he rushed past them along the verandah. A moment later, they heard him pounding up the stairs.

'What the Jupiter? What's he going up there for?' demanded Carotus. 'There's only the weaving room and winter bedrooms upstairs.'

'*Winter* bedrooms? Are there different bedrooms for winter?'

'Of course,' said Carotus. 'But . . .'

He broke off at the sound of cries and exclamations coming from the window above them.

'That's Valentia,' said Carotus, 'in the weaving room. What's going on?'

And now there was a babble of voices coming down the stairs.

Perry recognised Donata's voice, high and excited. 'I'm so proud of you, my husband. But it's so sudden. Only fourteen days to get ready!'

'Are we really going?' That was Valentia.

Maximus replied in a low rumble, then the three figures came out on the verandah. Valentia, still cuddling her kitten, danced along between her parents, but she stopped when she saw the boys.

'Wait,' she whispered to them, then she hurried after her parents into the office, and the door slammed shut behind her.

The boys stared at each other, then back at the solid wooden door.

'What's happening?' breathed Perry.

They waited, but there was no sign of Valentia.

Carotus looked at the knife in his hand.

'May as well get on with the trimming,' he said, 'and you can do watering.'

The citrons were planted in pots at the foot of every column and the boys had reached the far end of the courtyard when the door opened.

'Valentia!' shouted Perry and Carotus together, and they rushed to meet her as she flew down the path.

'You'll never guess!' she cried, laughing and excited. 'We're leaving Villa Rubia! I was up in the weaving room with Mother, when Father came up to tell us. The emperor's appointed him to be an official at the new imperial mint – that's a place where they make coins – and we're all going with him! We're leaving at the beginning of November!'

'U-us too?' stammered Carotus.

'Yes! You and Peregrinus are coming too because we need lots of slaves. We'll be living in a big, grand house in town.'

'Holy Jupiter!' said Carotus in an awed voice.

'And it's a really big town!' cried Valentia, dropping the kitten so she could fling her arms wide. 'Bigger than Forum Julii. Father says they have everything there: chariot-racing, gladiators—'

'*Gladiators?!*' exploded Carotus. With a huge grin he began to brandish his little knife like a sword.

Laughing, Valentia picked up a gardening fork. 'I can beat you!' she challenged.

'Come on, Peregrinus, find a weapon,' called Carotus.

But Perry could only stand stunned, hearing over and over the terrible words, 'We're leaving Villa Rubia. We're leaving Villa Rubia.'

'Noooo!' he wanted to wail. 'I can't leave here!'

He felt for the stylus, tucked in his belt, and gripped it tight.

It was only a matter of time before he came up with the word that would rescue him. One day, he would scratch something in the dirt and find himself in the ruins of the villa again, and he would run back over the vineyard to his family.

But he couldn't do that if he wasn't here!

'W-when did you say we're leaving?' he croaked.

'The first day of November,' carolled Valentia merrily.

That's only two weeks away! thought Perry.

If he didn't find a way home in two weeks, he'd be stuck in the past forever!

18

THE NEW PRESS

TILUVIMPUS BURST INTO THE COURTYARD carrying a bucket of water on his shoulder.

'Have they started the pressing?' cried Carotus, leaping to his feet.

'Any moment now.'

The water-carrier dumped the bucket in the nearest doorway and rushed back in the direction of the work buildings.

Perry pulled out the stylus from behind his back and began scribbling in the dirt again. This morning he'd had the brilliant idea of drawing a picture instead of writing.

But I wish I was better at drawing, he thought.

He scrubbed out the bonnet of the car and tried again.

Behind him, Carotus started dragging something, making loud scraping noises.

'Peregrinus, help me with this,' he called.

'Hang on . . .'

'*Eia*, crazy boy, did you hear me?!' cried Carotus. 'They're milling the olives and they'll be trying out the new press any moment. Come on!'

Perry raised his head and heaved a sigh.

'I had a good idea,' he mumbled, 'but it didn't work.'

'Come on. We're putting the citrons in the oilery to keep warm for winter.'

Reluctantly, Perry tucked his stylus in his belt. 'But aren't they busy in the oilery, getting the new press ready?'

'Exactly,' grinned Carotus. 'That's why this is the perfect time to do it! The pots have to be moved before we leave, and that's only two days away, so they can't complain. Come on, you lift the other side.'

When they reached the front of the villa, Poppillus was hurrying past, bringing loaves of bread for the slaves' dinner.

'Bit early, aren't you?' called Carotus.

'Better early than late,' retorted his grandfather, trotting towards the workyard.

'He's finding an excuse to get near the oil press too,' chuckled Carotus.

Perry stared at the loaves in Poppillus's basket, all scored ready to pull apart, and felt a lump rise in his throat.

The first time I saw bread like that, he thought, *was at the festival – nearly eight weeks ago!*

He remembered waiting under the hot sun while the loaves were pulled out of the pizza oven, and the sound of Mum's voice. *The Romans did not eat pizza.*

'Pizza!' he shouted. 'Hey, stop a minute.'

He dropped his side of the heavy pot, pulled out his stylus and started scratching in the hard clay surface.

P . . . I . . . Z . . .

'Forget about your stupid writing!' said Carotus impatiently. 'Come on, let's see the oil press.'

'I can't forget about it!' snapped Perry. 'If I don't . . .' He scrawled the last two letters, but he was not surprised when it didn't work.

'All right,' he sighed, and stood up again.

At that moment, Valentia came rushing out the gate from the workyard.

'There you are!' she cried. 'I've been waiting for you! Come on, they're starting.' She spun around, and raced back through the gate again.

The boys took one look at the pot, then abandoned it and chased after her.

The workyard was filled with noise, and the entrance to the oilery was jammed with excited onlookers. All the kitchen slaves were there, and Habita and Poppillus and Dannorix and Lollius . . .

'Let me through,' cried Valentia imperiously.

'And us,' said Carotus, diving in after her, and pulling Perry behind.

As they tumbled out the front of the crowd, Perry's eyes flew to the huge pressing beam that stretched the length of the room. At the end of it, standing upright like a column, was the giant screw.

Perry grinned.

The base of the screw was fastened by bolts to a weight stone – the stone with the extra hole in it.

Baskets of milled olives were stacked in a tower under the beam ready to be crushed. But nothing was happening. The farm manager and the head winemaker were standing next to Maximus, frowning at the new arrangement.

'I still can't see how it's going to work with a screw instead of a winch,' muttered the manager.

Maximus smiled. 'I assure you it does,' he said. 'This is how they do it in the north now.'

Two slaves stood waiting each side of the giant screw, hands resting on long wooden bars that jutted from it.

'All right, men, off you go!' said Maximus. 'Step together and push.'

The men moved in a circle, and as they moved, the wooden screw began to turn.

The manager thrust his hands on his hips. 'I can't see how going around in circles is going to press anything—' he began.

Then the whole crowd gasped. Slowly, with a lot of creaking and groaning, the massive weight stone began to rise from the ground.

'It's working!' shouted Carotus.

Everyone else was shouting and pointing too, and Valentia was laughing and clapping.

As the stone rose, the beam squeezed down on the baskets, and olive oil started oozing in a glistening stream through the woven reeds.

'That's it!' 'Look at the oil!' 'It's working!'

'Bet you've never seen anything as clever as that!' said Carotus, turning proudly to Perry.

But Perry didn't answer. With the stylus in his hand, he was backing out of the crowd.

Factory, machines, diggers! he thought excitedly.

19
GOODBYE

'CAROTUS, I'VE WORKED OUT THE problem!' cried Perry. 'Just in time! I've been writing in English and I should have been writing in Latin. After all, the stylus is Roman. I—'

'Take these out to the carriages,' said Carotus, thrusting a pile of scratchy woollen blankets into Perry's arms.

'Are you listening?' demanded Perry. Then he saw Gabrina come into the room and he stopped talking and hurried outside, carrying the blankets.

Today was the day of the departure. *But I'm not going with them*, thought Perry with relief. *I'm going back to my own time. I just need a chance to try my new idea.*

Three huge carriages and teams of mules filled

the entry yard, and Perry stared in astonishment at the things being loaded inside.

'What's that for?' he asked as Quintio and another boy heaved up a curved cushion as big as a couch.

'For picnicking on the road,' said Quintio.

Perry watched them pile in silver cups and round clay toilet pots, firewood and a grill, and even a small round table, then he shoved the blankets at them, and turned to race across the yard to the bakery.

Poppillus, with a large basket of bread, blocked his way.

'Here,' said the baker, 'these are the loaves for the slaves.'

Perry sighed in frustration, and turned around again.

Dannorix was peering into each carriage, checking the contents against a wooden notebook in his hands.

'Provisions?' he asked, seeing the basket on Perry's arm. 'Deposit that over there,' he instructed, pointing to the carriage at the back.

Each carriage was a huge wooden box with a driver's seat out the front, a curved roof, and an arched door opening in the middle. Perry dashed towards the last carriage, then stared, bewildered, through the doorway. The floor was level with his chest and there were no steps for climbing up.

Pushing the basket in first, he grabbed the edge of the floor and jumped and squirmed till he managed to hoist himself up. He staggered to his feet and looked around.

A plank bench was stretched across each end, facing the centre – and the whole middle of the floor was piled with food: wooden boxes of eggs, carefully nestled in straw, clay pots of honey and preserved pears, hunks of salted meat bound in wet vinegar-soaked cloths, linen sacks bulging with dried apples and figs, amphorae of wine and olive oil, raisins wrapped in fig leaves, strings of sausages and clay flasks of stinky fish sauce.

He dumped the bread on top, then jumped down.

This time, it was Bonica, the mistress's serving girl, who stopped him, pushing a silver jug and basin towards him.

'Hop up there, will you,' she said, nodding at the cart in front, 'and stow this safely.'

'But . . .'

'And this,' called someone else, passing up a wooden box. 'Be careful with it,' she warned. 'It's got glass bottles of hair oil and perfume inside.'

He looked out warily before he lowered himself down again, then sprinted across the yard.

Carotus was in their bedchamber, trying to drag out their box of clothes.

'Quick, tell me how to write "two thousand" in Roman numerals,' panted Perry.

'MM,' said Carotus, 'but—'

'Sssh.'

Perry knelt down and began to scratch furiously in the dirt floor. 'I'm writing the date from the future,' he explained. 'MMXX . . .'

He finished the last numeral, and looked up eagerly. 'Holy Jupiter,' he complained, copying his friend. 'I'm still here.'

'Yes, and now you can help me carry this,' said Carotus.

'Don't bother with my clothes,' Perry insisted as they staggered out the door. 'I won't be coming with you. I'm sure it's a Latin word . . . Hang on, I've got it!'

Without warning, he dropped his end of the box and knelt down again. '*Porta!*' he exclaimed. Gate, like gateway to the future . . .

But a few minutes later he was out in the yard, scowling as he helped manoeuvre their box of clothes into the middle cart.

Balbus and Habita were already inside, seated on one of the benches. Balbus's little face looked crumpled and anxious, but Habita was beaming.

'Valentia's just fetching her cat,' she said. 'We're nearly ready to leave! Sit down, son, and you,

Peregrinus, stop hopping around like a dog with fleas and take your seat.'

'No-o!' wailed Perry.

He rushed to the carriage door.

The master was just outside, giving last-minute instructions to his manager, and Valentia was bounding across the yard with Quintio behind her.

She collapsed against the carriage, panting for breath. 'Bucco ... wouldn't get in his basket,' she gasped. 'Come on, Quintio, put him in there, and help me up!'

Perry backed out of the way as she toppled in and lay on the floor, laughing and holding her sides. Then she stumbled to her feet and flopped on the bench beside Carotus.

'We're leaving!' she exclaimed. 'Come on, Peregrinus, come and sit here.' She patted the seat on the other side of her.

'No, I just ...' Perry sprang for the door again. He would jump down and run back ...

But the front carriage was already moving, and as Perry clutched the sides of the door, their driver leapt into his seat.

'Quick, sit down, you'll fall out,' called Valentia.

The yard was thronging with slaves as everyone who'd been left behind crowded around to shout goodbye.

'Goodbye!' Valentia yelled back, waving through the window.

Goodbye! That's it! That's the word! thought Perry. *When I wrote* Ave *– hello – I travelled to Roman times, so if I write* Vale *– goodbye – then I'll leave . . .*

He spun round, looking wildly for something he could scratch with his stylus. It didn't matter if everyone saw what he was doing. He just had to do it. Once he left the villa . . .

He fell on his knees, dragging the stylus from his belt. He would scratch on the wooden box.

'Peregrinus, what are you doing?' giggled Valentia.

The carriage jerked forward, and the tip of the stylus slipped as Perry tried to press it into the wood. He clutched it tighter and tried again. One side of the V . . .

'We're off to Arelate! We're off to Arelate!' sang out Valentia.

Perry froze.

'W . . . where did you say?' he stammered.

'Arelate. Didn't you know?' asked Valentia, smiling.

Perry stared at her. The words of his mum sounded in his head. 'The Latin name for Arles was *Arelate*,' she'd said, giving one of her tidbits.

'You mean . . .' He could barely speak. 'You mean, Arelate is the place where you're going to live?' he croaked.

'Of course,' chuckled Valentia. 'And you're going to live there too, silly.'

Perry felt as if the whole weight of a pressing beam was crushing down on him. If Valentia was going to live in Arles, then . . . then she *was* the girl from the stone coffin!

He heard the carriage ahead of them rumbling through the gate. This was it. This was his last chance. He could jump out now, write *Vale*, and get back to his own time. Or . . .

Their own carriage began to move.

If I don't jump now, it'll be too late, he thought. *I'll never see my family again.*

He stared at Valentia, clutching her precious cat basket, swaying and laughing. If he stayed with her, maybe he could do something to save her life. But if he left . . .

He knelt there for a long, agonising moment, the stylus pressed against the wood, then he shoved it back in his belt and stumbled across the rocking floor. As the carriage rolled out of the villa grounds, he dropped on the seat beside Valentia.

20

THE JOURNEY BEGINS

THE CARRIAGE RATTLED BETWEEN THE grapevines in a sea of crimson autumn leaves.

But Perry wasn't looking out the window. He was staring ahead, memories of his family pouring through his mind. He could see Melissa in the plane beside him, the two of them in a tiny pool of light, whispering and sharing a packet of peanuts, while everyone else slept around them ... He was remembering Mum at home, her face proud and beaming, handing him a strange-shaped jumper she had knitted for him ...

Mum, I'd wear every awful thing you ever made for me if only I could see you again, he thought, his eyes smarting with tears.

And he could see Dad, in shorts and bare feet, in the backyard, teaching him how to play totem tennis when he was little, and hitting the pole right out of the ground because he hadn't knocked it in far enough . . . Perry started to chuckle through his tears.

Valentia turned to him in surprise. 'Peregrinus, why—' she started to ask.

And then, 'The river,' shouted Carotus.

From beyond the grapevines came a glint of water.

Valentia leapt to her feet, throwing the cat basket onto Perry's lap.

'Careful,' warned Habita, as Valentia and Carotus rushed for the doorway.

Perry jumped up too, shoving the basket under the seat. The carriage was trundling closer and closer to the river . . .

There was a sharp jolt and Perry felt himself thrown against the wall. Water splashed and sloshed around them.

The mules are pulling us into the river! he thought.

Valentia shrieked, and his heart almost burst out of his chest. But she was still there, leaning out the door, hanging on with one hand, pointing and shouting to Carotus.

As Perry stared at her, he knew he could never have abandoned her, never have gone through the rest of his life imagining all the awful ways she might have died . . .

He stumbled forward and grabbed hold of her dress. 'Don't fall,' he pleaded.

She turned to him, her face sparkling with laughter. 'You're funny,' she snorted. 'This is the crossing place. We go this way to Forum Julii. Look, the water's so shallow, you could walk around in it.'

'Oh,' said Perry, giving her a wobbly smile.

Valentia dragged him between her and Carotus, and he looked down at the pebbles on the riverbed, and the shallow, clear water rippling through the wooden spokes in the wheels.

As the carriage lurched out the other side, the three of them hung onto each other, staggering back to their seat, and Perry found himself laughing with the others.

Valentia plonked herself next to the window and looked around for the cat basket.

'It's here,' said Perry, pulling it out from under the bench.

'It's getting too heavy,' said Valentia, pushing it away. 'Habita can hold it now.'

A few minutes later, they reached a wide, paved roadway.

'Forum Julii's to the left,' announced Valentia, then she bounced excitedly as the carriage swung in the opposite direction. 'I've never been this way before. Father said it will take us all the way to Arelate.'

'Look, children,' instructed Balbus, leaning over his fat stomach to peer out. 'This road is called Via Aurelia. It will take us all the way to Arelate.'

Valentia rolled her eyes. 'Deaf old Balbus,' she muttered.

A short, wide column stood alone by the road. Perry twisted back to look at it. Wasn't that . . . ? Yes! He'd seen that column before, only now it had the clear Roman numerals *XVIII* carved in the side of it, painted red.

'See that milestone?' he hissed to Carotus. 'It's still there in the future. I saw it when I drove here with . . .' His breath caught for a moment. 'With my family,' he finished.

'What are you two whispering about?' asked Valentia.

Perry and Carotus glanced at each other.

'He . . . I . . .' stammered Perry.

'Peregrinus wanted . . .' began Carotus.

An oxcart loaded with geese came lumbering towards them from the opposite direction, the noise of honking drowning out the boys' voices. As it passed, Perry glanced across to the other side of the carriage, and gave a startled shout.

'Look!' he sputtered, pointing out the doorway. 'Baskets with legs!'

The others looked, and fell back, roaring with

laughter. 'Baskets with legs!' they hooted. 'Baskets with legs!'

And now Perry saw there was a tiny, tubby donkey carrying the baskets. The animal's head was hanging low, while the baskets, strapped each side of him, were piled high with firewood. Perry started to laugh too, and the boy leading the donkey glanced up at the shrieking children as their carriage passed.

Balbus leaned forward, wagging his finger at them. '*Travel won't make a better man of you,*' he said, in his high, squeaky voice. '*For this we must spend time in study and the writings of wise men.*'

'It won't make a man of me at all!' squawked Valentia, and they all exploded into giggles again.

As the carriage travelled on, rattling and jolting over the stone-paved road, Balbus kept on reciting but none of them listened.

All at once, Perry jumped to his feet.

'Soldiers!' he shouted.

The carriage slowed to a halt, and the three children rushed to the doorway.

The front carriage had pulled up at an arched stone bridge guarded by soldiers, and Dannorix was waving a scroll out the window.

'He's showing them the pass,' said Valentia. 'It says Father's an important person, travelling with his entourage by command of the emperor!'

'Look at their swords and shields,' exclaimed Perry.

'And the helmets and spikes,' added Carotus.

'That's how I wanted to dress,' sighed Perry.

'You? What do you mean – you?' asked Valentia.

'Er . . .'

'Sometimes you say the strangest things,' said Valentia. 'Anyway, how come you're so excited about soldiers? You must have seen thousands up north, protecting the border.'

Perry stared at her blankly, but Carotus let out a yell. 'We're moving again!'

And now the vineyards and trees on both sides of the road gave way to buildings.

It's exactly like the pictures of Roman towns in the book! thought Perry.

Pale-coloured buildings lined the road, with bright, red-roofed verandahs and broad red stripes along the walls. Shops crowded the footpath, with contents spilling everywhere and counters open to the street.

'The town of Forum Voconii,' announced Balbus. 'Remember what the great Plutarch said . . .'

Perry gazed at the sausages sizzling over glowing embers, a baker pulling bread out of an oven, a man eating something that looked like hot fried fish wrapped in yellowish paper . . .

But no pizza, thought Perry sadly.

'I'm hungry,' declared Valentia. 'It must be nearly time for our picnic.'

She looked across at Habita.

'I don't think so, my little chick,' said the nursemaid.

Outside the town, there was a milestone with a red-painted *XXII* carved in the pillar.

'Ten-ten-two . . .' muttered Perry, working out the numeral. 'Twenty-two! So that means . . .' He subtracted the eighteen from the milestone near the villa. '. . . we've travelled four miles.'

'Is that all?' groaned Valentia. 'Father said we have to go twenty-three miles today!'

She slumped in her seat and glowered at the vineyards bordering the road again.

'I'm starving,' she grumbled.

For once, Balbus seemed to hear what she said. 'As the great Seneca wrote: *No journey can set you beyond the reach of cravings, fits of temper, or fears*,' he recited.

'Finally!' Valentia exclaimed, as the carriages turned off the main road and began to rock and bump down a track.

'We're going to overturn!' wailed Habita.

But they pulled up safely by the bank of a river.

Carotus jumped out and hobbled around rubbing his bottom. 'My legs are so stiff I can't feel them!' he laughed.

Perry slid carefully out of the carriage, holding the cat basket.

'How's my poor Bucco?' crooned Valentia, lifting the lid.

The little orange and white kitten was curled up, fast asleep.

'You cheeky thing!' she said. 'I was worrying about you the whole time!' She dropped the lid again and looked at Perry. 'Bring him over here. I'm going to see what they're cooking for us.'

Two hired men had come along to prepare the meals. One was holding up a large mixing bowl while the other added ingredients.

'Five ... six ... seven ...' he counted, cracking in the eggs.

'What are you making us?' asked Valentia.

'An omelette, miss.'

There was a *bump* inside the basket and Perry opened the lid. The kitten's head bobbed up, then he lifted his front paws onto the edge and looked inquisitively at the cook.

The man was beating the eggs with a wooden rod. He added olive oil, and slowly poured the mixture into a wide clay pan resting on a grill over the fire.

Perry breathed in happily as an enticing aroma wafted upwards, and the omelette turned golden and bubbly in the pan.

'Serving dish,' snapped the cook.

The other man held out a shiny red platter with shapes of antelopes and hares decorating the rim.

The cook heaped on the omelette, and then, to Perry's dismay, he added a drizzle of honey and a sprinkling of pepper.

'Ready!' he announced.

The picnic was set up among the trees with a red cloth draped across for a roof. Donata and Maximus lay on the large curved cushion, just like they did on their dining couch at home. Carotus set the huge omelette on a small round table in front of them and Valentia pulled up a folding stool.

She looked up at Perry and patted her knee. 'Here,' she said. 'Put Bucco on my lap.'

'Don't give that creature any food,' warned her father. 'He'll be sick in his basket.'

'Oh.' Valentia stroked the kitten for a moment, then lowered him to the ground. 'Never mind, Bucco. You run around instead.'

He sat up, miaowing hopefully, then began to sniff at the tall grasses waving over his head.

Valentia took a hunk of soft white bread and scooped up a generous portion of omelette. Perry's stomach gave a loud, hungry growl.

'Boys, you have my permission to eat,' said Maximus, waving his hand towards the river.

145

The slaves and hired men were lounging on the riverbank, having their own meal. Perry and Carotus bounded down to join them, then Perry groaned in disappointment. All they were eating was dry bread and figs.

He wandered around, scuffing at fallen leaves while he ate, and tossing a fig up and down. 'Here, catch,' he called to Carotus.

But it was soon time to pack up and leave.

'Let's get the roof down,' yelled Carotus. 'Race you!'

The red cloth was strung between two trees. Perry chose the higher tree and scrambled up as fast as he could. On the ground, everyone else bustled about, grabbing up the big curved cushion, the little table, the tray of preserved pears, the wine goblets . . .

As he loosened the cloth from the branches, Perry glanced at the other tree. Carotus was grinning, and pointing at Valentia standing below them, hands on hips, gazing around.

'One . . . two . . . three!' called Carotus quietly, and, at the same moment, both boys let the cloth drop.

It landed on Valentia's head.

'Don't,' she shrieked, struggling from under it and glaring up at them. 'Come down and look for Bucco,' she ordered. 'I can't find him.'

The boys slithered down and began to wander among the trees, calling the kitten's name.

Habita bustled up, carrying the cat basket.

'We have to go. Where's your cat?' she asked.

Maximus came striding over too. 'What's the delay?' he demanded.

'I can't find Bucco,' said Valentia, and Perry could hear a tremor in her voice.

'Wait, I know,' he cried.

He raced for the last carriage, where the provisions were loaded.

'Quick,' he called, leaning through the door, 'the master needs some garum.'

With a startled look, the cook picked up a flask, pulled out the lid, and passed it to him.

Trying not to breathe the smell, Perry went hurrying back.

'Here, this'll bring him,' he said. 'Hold out your hand.'

He poured on some fish sauce and the next second a little bundle of orange and white fur came bouncing towards them.

'Bucco!' cried Valentia, sweeping him into her arms. She giggled as his tongue licked her fingers.

'I didn't realise a cat would cause me so much trouble when I brought one home with me,' said Maximus when they headed back to the carriage. But his eyes were twinkling.

He leaned in the door as they settled into their seats.

'Keep the lid tight on that cat basket!' he cautioned. 'We've still got a long way to go. This'll be the biggest journey any of you children have ever been on.'

As he strode off, Valentia turned a puzzled face to Perry.

'Why did Father say this is the biggest journey you've ever been on?' she asked.

As he stared back at her, not speaking, her eyes widened.

'You've been keeping a secret, haven't you? I don't believe you come from Augusta Treverorum at all! Where *do* you come from?'

The carriage began to lurch and rattle up the track again. Perry took a deep breath and glanced at Carotus. 'Will I tell her?' he asked.

'Tell me what?' exclaimed Valentia.

'Sssh,' hissed Carotus. He looked at Habita. But she was talking to Balbus on the other side of the carriage. He leaned forward with a huge grin on his face. 'Go on, mystery boy, tell her,' he said.

21

THE SECRET

'TELL ME WHAT?' VALENTIA DEMANDED again, and she looked with impatience from one boy to the other.

Perry was bursting with excitement now. He bent close to her ear.

'You're right,' he whispered. 'I do come from somewhere else. I come from the future!'

For one instant, Valentia looked at him in amazement, then she crossed her arms and glared. 'Now tell me the truth,' she snapped.

'It *is* true!' squawked Carotus, bubbling with laughter. 'I didn't believe him either, but he proved it. Go on, Peregrinus, tell her more.'

On the other side of the carriage, Balbus began his recital again. '*Can wisdom, then, the greatest art of all, be picked up in the course of taking a trip?'* he declaimed.

But the children ignored him, huddling together, their heads close.

'How can it be true?' Valentia's whisper was shrill with astonishment. 'How did you get here? How did it happen?'

Perry thought back to that moment, two months before, when he'd found the stylus. 'In the future,' he said slowly, 'Villa Rubia is a ruin . . .'

'A ruin!' protested Valentia.

'Yes, and that's . . .'

Valentia listened, gasping, as Perry told his story.

'So . . . you just happened to arrive the day Father came back from the north?' she asked at last.

'Yes!'

'That's so funny.' She burst into chuckles. 'Everyone at the villa thought you travelled in the carriages with him.'

'But I don't understand why your father never asked where I came from,' said Perry. 'He must have known I didn't arrive with him.'

Valentia shrugged. 'He was away for three years. He probably thought you were just one of the little slaves around the villa who'd got bigger.'

Carotus was almost jumping off his seat with impatience. 'Tell her about the future, Peregrinus.

Tell her about carriages that move by themselves,' he demanded. 'And—'

'Carriages can't move by themselves,' scoffed Valentia.

'They can in the future,' said Perry. 'And they go so fast we can travel from Villa Rubia to Arelate in two hours. We even have carriages that can fly, and—'

'And you're not going to believe about the slaves,' crowed Carotus. 'Tell her about the slaves.'

Perry grinned. 'There aren't allowed to be slaves anymore,' he said. 'I'm not a slave in the future.'

Valentia stared. 'There have to be people to light fires and cook and serve and everything,' she said. 'Or are you going to say you have carriages that do that too?'

They all burst into giggles.

Then Valentia grew solemn again. 'Some people have to be slaves,' she insisted. 'They're born that way.'

Perry looked at Carotus. 'Is that how you got to be a slave?'

'Of course. My mother was a slave, so I am too.'

'But . . . I can't understand why you aren't angry about it,' said Perry. 'Don't you want to be free, like those men who came to pick the grapes?'

Carotus shook his head. 'Those men have a rotten life. They have to hire themselves out for any job they can get, and even then they're starving half the time. At least I have enough to eat, and I have a master who doesn't whip his slaves . . .'

'And you get to have lessons,' added Valentia.

Carotus rolled his eyes.

'But, Carotus, you shouldn't *have* a master,' protested Perry. 'There shouldn't *be* someone who's allowed to whip you!'

The three of them hardly noticed the road they were rattling along as they went on arguing and questioning in low voices. It was only when they heard shouting, and felt the carriage veer sharply, that they looked up.

They had turned down a narrow road with posts, like gateposts, on either side.

The words 'PRIVATE ROAD' were carved into the stone.

'We've arrived!' cried Carotus. 'This must be the villa where we're staying tonight.' And then, 'Holy Jupiter,' he gasped as the gardens and house came into view.

Perry had thought Villa Rubia was grand, but this one was about three times the size. And the garden in front of it was like a park.

'Look at those trees,' Valentia burst out, pointing at some topiary bushes pruned in the shapes of animals.

'And there's a lake with a whole island on it,' exclaimed Perry.

'This belongs to a friend of Father's,' said Valentia, with a note of pride in her voice.

'The master must have made important friends at the emperor's court,' said Carotus, 'if they live in places like this.'

Inside was even more impressive. Dinner was served in a dining hall as big as a basketball court. Statues painted in bright colours with highlights of gold stood in niches around the walls, and a mosaic of hunters on horseback decorated the floor. But most amazing of all, in the middle of the room, was a real pond with real fish in it.

Perry and Carotus stood behind their master and mistress, buffeted and bumped by the flock of slaves hurrying about.

'I hope Bucco doesn't try to eat the fish in the pond,' said Perry, glancing anxiously at the kitten on Valentia's lap.

But the kitten was more interested in the fancy platters of food – wild boar, fried lobster, and a peacock served in its own green and blue feathers.

Next morning, when they met in the carriage again, Valentia was bubbling with excitement. 'Isn't this place amazing?' she exclaimed. And then she looked smug. 'Father said our house in town is going to be really grand too. Peregrinus, what's your house in the future like? Do you have statues and a pond in your dining room?'

Perry burst out laughing. 'Definitely not! And we don't have fancy mosaic pictures on the floor either.'

'So . . .' Valentia frowned. 'You're very poor then?'

'No, just normal,' said Perry. 'That's how normal people live.'

'Tell her about the tablets you write on with your fingers,' prompted Carotus, 'and the little boxes where you can talk to people far away.'

That evening they stayed at a smaller villa, but the next morning as they headed for the carriages, the boys overheard Maximus speaking worriedly to his wife.

'It's a pity we have to stay at an inn tonight,' he sighed. 'It's not really suitable for you and Valentia. I'm afraid there'll be some rowdy and unsavoury characters there.'

'What did he mean?' asked Perry, as they clambered into the carriage.

'I don't know, but I can't wait to find out,' chortled Carotus.

Night was falling by the time they reached the inn. The carriages rolled through a wide gate into a courtyard, and Carotus and Perry peered eagerly through the window. Flickering lights danced out of the darkness as boys, with oil lamps dangling on sticks, darted forward to unhitch the mules and lead them to the stables.

Jumping from the carriage, Perry and Carotus looked around for the rowdy, unsavoury characters.

'Carotus, Peregrinus,' called Habita, hustling Valentia towards a door. 'Don't loiter. Follow me.'

They stepped into a confusion of noise and arms and legs and shouting faces, people knocking over chairs, howling, arguing, waving things in the air. There was a stink of smoke and wine and strange food.

Perry stared in astonishment. Carotus beamed with glee.

'I think we've found them!' Carotus yelled in Perry's ear.

Then Perry jumped as a man beside him slammed his fist on a tabletop and bellowed in anger. Dice flew off the table, and pottery mugs crashed on their sides, spattering Perry with their stinky contents.

'Go outside if you want to fight,' shouted a man from across the room.

But the men at the table ignored him.

'You cheating scumbag!' snarled the one nearest Perry. He had bulging red cheeks and a squashed nose.

'It was a two not a three,' shouted the other.

Bit of a rough game, thought Perry, edging away.

155

A burst of noise came from the other side of the room, where men and women lolled on benches, swigging from big pottery mugs. They were trying to sing, waving their arms around as they warbled. The women looked strange, their faces painted white and their cheeks bright red.

Behind them, Maximus and Donata were being ushered into a side chamber. Perry glimpsed Valentia turning back to stare over her shoulder with wide, astonished eyes before she followed them inside.

'Come on, let's eat,' said Carotus, pushing Perry towards a crowded dining table.

They squeezed onto the end of a bench and Perry looked with dismay at the half-eaten platters of food, gnawed bones and nutshells scattered in front of him.

To his left, the men were starting their dice game again. The man with the broken nose rolled his dice and gave a snort of disgust, blowing out a bubble of snot.

'I don't like this place,' muttered Perry.

'I do,' grinned Carotus.

22

ARELATE

'EVERYONE UP, THE MASTER WANTS an early start,' yelled Dannorix.

Perry groaned. He didn't want to wake up. He was dreaming about being at home, bouncing on the couch with his friends, cheering and shouting as they watched the Grand Final on TV together . . .

He screwed his eyes shut, trying to stop the dream from slipping away.

'Peregrinus, I saw something funny last night,' Carotus murmured in his ear.

'It's too early in the morning for jokes,' grumbled Perry.

Carotus ignored him. 'While you were sleeping, there were mice crawling all over you!'

Perry shot off the straw mattress to the floor, his eyes flying open.

'Well, there was one mouse, anyway,' chuckled Carotus.

Fresh mules were harnessed to the carriages, and at dawn they were rumbling out of the courtyard, back onto Via Aurelia.

Perry stared sleepily at the walls of a town rearing up just beyond the inn. He hadn't noticed it in the dark the evening before.

'Children, this is the town of Aquae Sextiae,' announced Balbus as they trundled through the entrance gate. 'It was one of the first towns founded by the Romans in . . .'

'Aquae Sextiae!' exclaimed Perry, suddenly fully awake. He turned to his friends.

'I've been here before,' he confided in a low voice.

Memory washed over him: their hire car in a sunlit, cobbled square, the taste of flaky croissant, Mum glancing from the front seat to tell them one of her tidbits: 'The Roman name for Aix was Aquae Sextiae . . .' He gulped and went on hastily. 'It's only an hour from Arelate. We're nearly there.' And then he let out a huff. 'Oh no, I keep forgetting. In my time we drove the whole way from Arelate to your villa in a couple of hours. I can't believe it's taking us days and days to get back.'

The streets were already busy. Porters with loads on their backs trudged ahead of them along the road. Hawkers wandered about shouting their wares, slaves crowded around a carved stone fountain filling buckets of water, and donkeys, tied to the kerbstones, brayed noisily and nipped at everyone who passed.

'Tell us what it was like when you were here, Peregrinus,' whispered Valentia.

Perry stared through the window but now he wasn't seeing the scene outside. He was remembering cafe tables, the coldness of a *limonade* straight from the fridge, his sister snapping photos.

He blinked. A grand, colonnaded building was coming into focus outside the window, and some sort of market . . .

Then the rattle of the carriage wheels and the *clip-clop* of the mules' hooves grew louder and faster. They were leaving the town behind.

'We're on our way!' sang out Valentia.

Perry turned to look at her.

'When's your birthday?' he asked.

'My birthday?' Valentia looked surprised. 'On the Ides of November. In ten days. Why? Are you going to buy me a big present?' She grinned to show she didn't really mean it.

'I . . . I just wondered if we'd be in Arelate by then,' he lied.

'Oh, only just!' she exclaimed. 'Father said it'll take us nearly four more days to get to Arelate.'

'Four more days,' groaned Carotus.

Perry wasn't thinking about the journey, though. He was worrying about the writing on the coffin, and working out that in two months and eleven days, if he didn't save her, Valentia would be dead.

But I will *save her!* he promised himself.

The last morning of their journey finally arrived. As the carriage rattled down the last stretch to Arelate, the children hung out the window – Perry holding tight to Valentia – and they all scanned the road ahead.

'There it is!' cried Carotus. 'I saw it first!'

But they could all see it: a high stone wall encircling a hill, an imposing entrance with archways and tall, round towers, a queue of carts waiting to get in . . . and then, before they even reached the gate, a tumble of people, buildings, noises and smells that had spilled out of the city and spread along the road.

'Peuw, what's that pong?' squawked Carotus admiringly.

Perry stared at some men dipping animal skins in a vat of foul-looking liquid, and swilling it around.

Then he caught a glimpse of sheep lining up at a huge shed. There was lots of bleating, and stamping and splashing . . . and blood.

'That looks fun,' said Carotus, but to Perry's relief he didn't mean the sheep getting slaughtered. Carotus was craning out to watch a potter, smeared in clay up to his elbows, shaping a giant amphora.

'What's going on over there?' asked Valentia.

A crowd of people were parading along, blowing flutes and horns, while others carried a long stretcher heaped with flowers. Smoke and incense drifted behind them.

'That's a dead body under those flowers!' cried Carotus.

'Yes, it's a funeral,' said his mother.

Perry's stomach gave a sickening lurch as he noticed the tombs crowded on both sides of the road. He'd seen a few of them outside the other towns, but here there were hundreds of them.

That's where the stone coffins in the museum came from, he realised in dismay.

But now their carriage was racketing past the queue of waiting carts, and they could see Dannorix hanging out his window with the special pass. The soldiers on guard waved them towards the big central archway.

'It's fun being important!' declared Valentia.

'We enter Arelate, the "little Rome" of Gaul,' burbled Balbus.

The children gazed up at the massive wall and solid towers looming over them.

'They look as if they could last forever,' said Valentia in awe.

'They do,' whispered Perry. 'Some of them are still there in my time.'

He blinked. The last time he'd seen that wall he'd been with his family . . .

The carriages fought their way along a road milling with pedestrians. There were people everywhere – crowding up to shop counters, flowing off the footpaths, shouting greetings to each other, and stopping to chat or barter.

'There must be *thousands* of people living in Arelate,' exclaimed Carotus.

'Of course there are,' snorted Perry. 'It's a city!'

And then, 'Look over there,' cried Valentia and Carotus together.

Two gigantic circular buildings were coming into view on the road ahead. They seemed to grow larger and larger as the carriages trundled towards them.

'That one's the amphitheatre,' shouted Perry. 'That's where the gladiators fight!'

Habita shot him a surprised glance, and he hastily dropped his voice. 'That's still around in my time too,' he muttered, but now he was bursting with excitement. He might see real gladiators this time, not just an empty ruin!

Balbus pointed at the building opposite. 'Ah, a theatre,' he exclaimed. 'Look, children, notice how only the front is curved. The back is straight for the scenery and stage. I trust we will see a play here by Seneca . . .'

Perry saw Carotus and Valentia roll their eyes at each other. Seneca was one of the boring writers the tutor was always quoting.

The carriages turned right into a side street.

'We're heading towards the river,' whispered Perry. 'The place where we stayed was down this way.'

'There are no trees,' complained Carotus.

Perry looked up and down the street and realised he hadn't seen a glimmer of a garden since they'd come through the entrance gate. Buildings were crammed together along the road, with houses and shops opening straight off the footpath.

'We're here!' yelled Valentia as the carriages slowed, and the next moment they were pulling up outside a large, grand-looking building.

'This is it!' breathed Valentia.

'Come on!' cried Carotus.

The master and mistress were already alighting from their carriage.

Leaping to the ground, Carotus held out his hand to Valentia, and Perry scrambled after them.

Maximus and Donata were waiting under the

porch and Donata turned to them with a delighted smile, drawing Valentia to her side.

Perry gaped at the brightly painted columns decorating the front of the house. Under their feet, the footpath was paved in marble, while the upper storey jutted over their heads. Stone carvings of strange animals with lion heads and wings framed the entrance, and the pair of front doors were the grandest Perry had ever seen – big solid panels studded with bronze nail heads.

'Imagine what it will be like inside!' whispered Carotus.

Everyone had piled out of the carriages now, and gathered behind their master.

Dannorix, standing by the door, looked back enquiringly.

Maximus gave a nod.

Dannorix turned and hammered the panels with his fist. 'Open up, doorman! The master of the household has arrived!' he bellowed.

23

TOWN HOUSE

AS THE DOORS BEGAN TO open Perry had a glimpse of two men inside, then Maximus strode forward, cloak swinging. The next instant all Perry could see was a crowd of people filling the entrance. He and Carotus rushed to join them, but they had to jig up and down, waiting impatiently, till the more important people had gone through first.

At last it was the boys' turn. They stepped into a long, narrow room, lit only by a few bronze oil lamps on stands along the walls.

Half-lit by the flickering flames, the two men waited at one side to greet the new arrivals. One of them was tall and thin, the other shorter, with broad shoulders. They both looked much grander than any of the servants at Villa Rubia. They wore coloured leggings and tunics with elaborate decorations on the sleeves and hems.

The short man stood to attention while everyone passed – *the doorman,* thought Perry – but the other man spoke to each arrival in greeting. When the boys drew near, he eyed them keenly under his beetling black brows. He had a lean, clean-shaven face, swarthy skin, black hair, and a long nose with flaring nostrils.

'He looks like a mule,' Carotus murmured to Perry, and the two of them were sniggering as they reached him.

'I am Urbinus, the steward,' he glowered. 'And you two need to smarten up. I don't tolerate monkeys in this house.'

As the steward strode off to join Maximus at the front of the procession, Carotus pulled a face at his back.

'Mule-face,' he muttered.

'I can hear a fountain,' said Perry.

Carotus listened.

'You're right, I bet that's the courtyard garden over there,' he said, pointing at a pool of light ahead of them.

But when they reached it, it was not a garden. It was a vast room with sunlight shining through a square hole in the roof, onto a pond of gleaming marble. The room had grand decorations everywhere:

carved and painted columns holding up the roof, a pattern of black-and-white mosaics all over the floor . . . But not a single tree, not even a citron in a pot, and the fountain was just a stone urn trickling water in the pond.

People were starting to move away, disappearing down corridors in all directions.

'Let's look in there,' said Perry, pointing at a huge dining room on the other side of the pond. The floor of it seemed alive with the writhing figures of beasts and gods made of coloured mosaic tiles.

They were just about to step through the wide double doors when someone grabbed them by the backs of their tunics.

'What do you monkeys think you're up to?' snapped Urbinus. 'Take yourselves to the kitchen. Be off with you.'

He shoved them towards a narrow corridor on the far side of the house.

'Huh,' said Carotus, and he jerked his tunic straight before he stalked away.

But when they reached the corridor, he stopped and looked to left and right in puzzlement.

'This house is crazy,' he exclaimed. 'The rooms are all over the place.'

Perry chuckled. It was the villa that had been weird, with all its rooms opening off the courtyard. 'This house is normal!' he said.

'Well, which way are we supposed to go then?' demanded Carotus.

In front of them, inside a smallish room, they could see Valentia, her back to them, sitting with her parents. To the right were a couple more rooms, but no sign of a workyard.

'Let's try down here,' suggested Perry, turning left.

Boxes and baskets from the carriages had been piled along the corridor. As Carotus edged his way past, Perry glanced down a tiny hallway on his right.

'Look!' he exclaimed, grabbing Carotus by the sleeve. 'Indoor toilets!'

'Don't be silly …' Carotus began, and then he, too, turned to look.

There were two doors opening off the tiny hall. Through one, they could clearly see a long wooden seat with two holes in it. From the other drifted the smell of cooking and the chatter of voices. Carotus took a step closer.

'What the Jupiter?!' he exclaimed. 'The kitchen's in here too.'

There were pots steaming on a stove, and people, including Habita, seated around a table.

'Come on,' cried Carotus.

Perry listened eagerly as Carotus bent down to his mother.

'What's the kitchen doing in here?' Carotus

inquired in a low, excited voice. 'Why isn't it out in the workyard?'

'Town houses don't have yards,' Habita answered.

'What?!'

'Sshh,' murmured Habita, and Perry saw her cast an embarrassed glance at three pretty girls sitting on her other side.

The girls, who looked about fourteen, acted as if the new arrivals didn't exist. They just went on gossiping together and fiddling with their long blond hair. They all wore dresses with colourful decorations stitched around their necks and sleeves.

Mule-face Urbinus appeared in the doorway. 'The master is ready for his meal,' he called.

Carotus straightened quickly and looked around. Someone was holding up a platter of white bread. But before Carotus could take it, the three pretty girls rose to their feet.

Carotus gasped, and Perry felt his own jaw drop. Now that the girls were standing up, it was obvious they weren't girls at all! Their tunics were the wrong length. They were boys with long hair.

Urbinus nodded to them. 'Secundus, Arro, Vibius, off you go,' he said.

Perry saw two red spots flare on Carotus's cheeks as the blond boys took the bread, relish, water and wine and paraded out of the room.

Perry moved to his friend's side. 'Maybe it's just for today,' he soothed. 'When Urbinus knows who you are . . .'

At the sound of their muttering, Mule-face glared at them, wagging his finger. 'You two will have to prove you can serve in an elegant manner before I give you that privilege. For now, you can spend your time being attendants and polishing silver. You can accompany the master to the bathhouse, and attend Valentia when she goes to school.'

Perry turned, beaming, to Carotus. 'School! That's better than being a slave!' he said.

But Carotus looked furious. He dropped on the seat the blond boys had vacated and dragged Perry down beside him.

'What about looking after the courtyard garden and making garlands for the shrine?' he growled at his mother. 'Do I get to do that at least?'

'Town houses don't have gardens either, dear,' said his mother sadly. 'The flowers for the shrine will come from the market.'

No garden! But then there'll be nowhere to play footy! thought Perry. *Even if we get hold of a ball.*

A finger prodded him in the back.

He glanced around. A slave girl was standing behind him with some clothes in her arms.

'Urbinus said these are for you two boys to put

on after your bath,' she said. 'They used to belong to Vibius and Secundus.'

Carotus eyed them with disgust.

'I'll hold them while you finish eating, dear,' said his mother in her cosiest voice.

But Perry and Carotus only had time for a few bites of lentils and pickled turnips before Mule-face was ordering them around again.

'Time to go to the bathhouse,' he called.

To Perry's astonishment, nearly every man and boy in the kitchen immediately jumped to his feet.

With an annoyed grunt, Carotus took the tunic and a pair of leggings his mother held out to him.

'I can't wear these,' cried Perry, looking at the clothes Habita put in his hands.

There were pink leggings, a bright blue tunic with big purple circles woven in the shoulders and skirt, and . . .

'Are these really boys' clothes?' he demanded, dangling a pair of soft black shoes by their ankle ties.

'You'll look very fine, both of you,' said Habita. 'Now hurry up, they're leaving. Grab your bath tools from your box. It's in the corridor.'

Carotus was still scowling as he and Perry trailed after the crowd. 'They can't possibly squeeze so many people into a bathhouse,' muttered Carotus.

24

BATHHOUSE

'I THINK I KNOW WHERE we're going!' cried Perry as everyone began to file out the front door.

The master was climbing into a strange small carriage – rather like a curtained four-poster bed – that rested on the ground by the side of the road.

'Ah, a sedan chair,' warbled Balbus. 'Very proper for a man of his status.'

'One ... two ... up!' shouted a voice, and Maximus was swayed into the air, like a pigeon on a spit, as four men grasped the poles jutting out front and back and hoisted the bed-chair onto their shoulders.

They all began to walk in procession up the road.

'What's happening?' demanded Carotus. 'I thought we were supposed to be having a bath.'

'We are!' grinned Perry. 'I bet we're going to Constantine's bathhouse!'

'Don't be silly. Constantine's the emperor. We can't use his bathhouse.'

'Yes we can. He built it for everyone. I read about it, and we passed it when I was here with my family. My mother said we're going to visit it after . . . ' His voice trailed away.

'Hey, you aren't wearing your blue underthing, are you?' Carotus asked anxiously.

'No, it's packed at the bottom of our box.'

As they turned the corner, the street grew busy and noisy. People hurried along with bath tools, towels and boxes of clothes, sedan-chairs lurched overhead, and hawkers rushed in and out, shouting and waving goods in the air.

'Cough cures! Get your cough cures here!' called a boy, lifting a small clay bottle from a basket around his neck. 'Horse saliva!' he cried encouragingly. 'Just drink it with hot water.'

Perry watched in astonishment as a man held out a coin.

'This cure's better!' cackled a bent old woman, shoving a handful of something pale and powdery under the man's nose. 'Pigeon dung – gargle it with raisin wine,' she instructed. 'Best remedy for a sore throat.'

'Carotus, do people really drink this stuff?' Perry demanded.

Carotus shrugged. 'My mother uses ground millipedes mixed in vinegar and honey,' he said.

Perry stared at him.

'But . . .' And then an awful thought struck him. Was that how Valentia was going to die? By drinking millipedes – or horse spit? Or pigeon dung?!

Maximus leaned out the window of his chair. 'Balbus! There's the school where you'll take Valentia,' he called.

Perry shoved away his worries – *If Valentia gets sick, I won't let her drink any of their cures*, he thought – and turned to look.

Beside them was a row of shops with columns along the front, and a hubbub of customers at open counters.

'That's not a school,' he said.

'Do you know what school is?' asked Carotus.

'Of course. I've been going to school since I was five. It's a place where lots of children have lessons together.'

The two of them peered, baffled, at the row of shops. They could see a woman selling squawking hens and live rabbits – *I guess they're for eating*, thought Perry – and a brassware stall where a boy was noisily banging a stick inside a jug to attract customers. There was a sweaty, red-faced pastrycook shovelling pies from an oven, a cobbler hammering a pair of shoes . . .

'But no school,' insisted Perry. Then he scanned along the road and spotted a huge stripy building on the corner. 'Constantine's Bathhouse!' he said excitedly. 'I told you.'

The bathhouse looked just the way he remembered it. The walls were built in bright, contrasting layers of pale stone and dark red brick, and it had a curved section like a fat stomach jutting towards the road.

They waited at the entrance while Dannorix handed over a few coins, then they all filed into a huge courtyard. Men and boys, wearing nothing but bits of cloth around their hips, were jogging barefoot around the yard, and . . .

'They're playing ball,' cried Perry, grabbing Carotus's arm. 'Look! Let's—'

But Urbinus caught them by their tunics again, and pushed them towards a room on their left.

'Undress before you do anything else,' he growled.

The room had carved wooden shelves to store their clothes on, and everyone was handed a linen towel to tie around their hips.

'Go for a run or play some ball before you bathe,' ordered Mule-face.

Balbus must have heard, for he nodded approvingly. '*A healthy mind in a healthy body*,' he intoned.

Back in the courtyard, Vibius, Arro and Secundus were standing in a triangle, throwing and catching a ball to each other.

'Let's show them how to play footy,' cried Perry, darting forward.

'I don't think . . . ' Carotus began.

But Perry snatched the ball and backed off, laughing. The ball was made of brown leather and felt solid, as if it was filled with stuffing instead of air.

'Catch!' he yelled, and gave the ball a wallop with his bare foot. 'Woohoo!' he cheered as it sailed straight at Carotus.

'Kick it back!' Perry hollered, skipping sideways and waving his arms.

Carotus poked his tongue out at the others, then tried.

The ball dribbled off the side of his foot and Perry threw himself on top of it, his bones jarring on the hard marble paving. He bounded to his feet again, laughing and exhilarated, but the other boys were just standing, staring, like statues.

'You have to get it back,' Perry yelled at them.

Vibius sprang to life then, hurling himself at Perry. 'You can't do that. It's our ball!' he shrieked.

Perry danced out of the way and the bigger boy crashed to the ground.

Laughing, Perry wove and dodged across the courtyard with the others racing after him. 'Come on,' he teased, calling over his shoulder.

Carotus was running too, waving his arms and shouting. In moments they tumbled in a heap on the ground, writhing, kicking and punching, with Carotus on top, yelling insults.

'Buffoons, weasels, snake-faces,' he sang out.

'What are you boys up to?' thundered a voice.

Thrashing arms and legs were dragged apart, and Perry saw a purple-faced Urbinus glaring down.

'You're all a disgrace to the house of Maximus,' he bellowed. 'Give me that ball and go have your baths.'

Perry and Carotus followed the others back to the dressing room, Carotus still spitting insults. Vibius, Arro and Secundus headed for a row of strange-looking shoes on a shelf and began to tug them on.

'What are those for?' whispered Perry, staring at the chunks of wood with leather straps the boys were sliding onto their feet.

'Don't know,' shrugged Carotus, 'but we'd better put some on too.'

'This feels funny,' chuckled Perry, trying to walk around on the big lumps of wood.

Carotus was thumping his as noisily as he could

on the mosaic floor. 'Let's find the baths,' he said, and he led the way to the door at the end of the room, where the blond boys had disappeared.

They stepped through the door and gazed around in amazement. A vaulted ceiling soared over their heads, and emerald-tinged glass in hundreds of little panes sparkled in the windows.

Carotus pointed at the circular swimming pools set in the floor at each end of the hall.

'Look how big they are!' he squawked.

'We have bigger ones in the . . . ' Perry started to say. Then stopped. The men splashing around in the water had no clothes on.

Those aren't swimming pools, he realised. *They're baths for washing in!*

'This really is an emperor's bathhouse,' said Carotus in an awed voice.

Perry nodded. This was nothing like the little slave bath at Villa Rubia, where only two people could fit in at once. There had to be at least fifty people in each of these baths.

Carotus dipped his fingers in the water. 'Cold,' he stated. 'Let's find a hot bath.'

They began to cross the hall, heading for an arched doorway. Under their feet, their wooden soles clattered on gleaming slabs of green and white stone, and all around, staring down from the top of pedestals, were statues. Perry stared back at them. The statues he'd seen in the Arles museum had faded to boring, bare stone, but the ones in the past were alive with colour. He passed a pink, muscly god, dressed in a yellow lionskin and brandishing a giant club, and a goddess in a long, red-painted robe with a snake over her shoulder.

Between the statues, men were stopping to chat.

'Wash well,' called one of them, raising his right hand to greet someone joining the group.

'Wash well,' the other one responded.

Perry smothered a laugh. It sounded funny, saying hello like that.

The next hall ponged of oil and perfume. It was furnished with elegant wooden chairs and beds, and men were lolling about, rubbing on oil – or being oiled by their slaves.

'Hang on, isn't that . . . ?'

Perry grabbed Carotus by the arm and both boys stared at a man sitting on a chair, having his cheeks patted with oil by the barber. The man looked very strange. Half his face was deeply tanned, but his newly shaven chin was shiny white . . .

'It's the master,' gasped Carotus.

The barber held up a mirror, but Maximus brushed him aside and stood up.

'Come on,' cried Carotus.

Giggling and rushing, the boys gave themselves a quick splash of oil and hurried into the next room, after the master. This was the grandest room of all. It was lit by towering windows, and shafts of sunlight shone on steam that rose from three gigantic hot baths. A sparkling stream of water ran into a stone basin carved like a seashell, and there were gilded statues and painted columns everywhere.

As they picked their way through the steam, Perry could feel the heat radiating up through the floor.

Now I know what these wooden shoes are for, he thought.

Maximus had chosen a large round pool, and they could see him sitting there, naked, getting boiled a bright pink colour, while he talked to his friends. A bunch of slaves waited behind them, holding their masters' silver bath tools and towels.

Perry jerked his head at a different bath. 'Let's get in that one,' he yelled, fighting to make himself heard over the din of shouting bathers.

They threw their towels on the floor and hopped down to the stone seat that ran around the edge.

'A-ah,' said Carotus, sliding down till the water lapped over his chin.

But Perry held himself up as tall as he could. 'Eww!' he complained, looking around at the scummy surface with bits of hair floating around. 'This is disgusting!'

Carotus grinned, then splashed some in Perry's face.

'Yuck!' squawked Perry, and he immediately kicked his feet, so that waves poured over Carotus's head.

'War!' yelled Carotus, and before Perry could catch hold of the side, Carotus plunged down and dragged him off the seat by the ankles.

The next moment, both boys were thrashing around in the warm water.

'Yuck, it's getting in my mouth,' wailed Perry, but he was laughing too.

By the time they got back to the dressing room, Vibius, Secundus and Arro were dressed again, and making a big show of brushing their long hair with combs made of bone.

Perry and Carotus turned their backs on them and began to pull on their hand-me-down clothes.

'Hey, check this out. Bet this corn-head's never worn leggings before,' jeered Vibius, as Carotus hopped around, trying to get his leggings untwisted.

All the blond boys rolled around laughing.

'Well, you peacock-feathers can't play ball,' growled Carotus.

A few minutes later, the whole household was ready to leave.

The master was clothed in a new tunic of bright scarlet, appliquéd with woven panels of horses and archers. He had a full-length cloak fastened at one shoulder by a gold brooch, a broad belt around his waist, and a signet ring glittering on his hand.

'Fitting garb for an officer of the Imperial Mint,' murmured Dannorix.

Maximus climbed into his sedan chair again, and they made a grand procession leaving the bathhouse. Perry grinned and waved to the people making way for them, but Carotus pulled a face at a little girl watching with her thumb in her mouth.

They headed back the way they'd come, and Perry peered again at the cages of hens and rabbits, the pastrycook and the cobbler's. This time, he noticed stone steps between them, leading upwards.

'Hey,' he said, 'I think the school might be up those stairs.'

He looked back as they walked on, searching eagerly for a sign of a child or a teacher in the windows upstairs. But there was no movement at all.

'I can't wait to see what school here is like,' said Perry. 'I hope our teacher is better than Balbus!'

25

SCHOOL

'OFF TO SCHOOL!' PERRY sang out.

He pulled his cloak tighter, shivering with cold and excitement. He was glad now he had those pink leggings to wear.

'Brr, it's freezing,' gasped Valentia.

Carotus bumped roughly into Perry. 'Sorry, couldn't see you, too dark!' he snorted.

Laughing, Perry bumped him back.

Classes began at sunrise, and the street, as they hurried along, was almost pitch black. But Balbus was waddling in front of them, an oil lamp dangling from chains in his hands, casting a pool of light.

'Look at my breath,' chuckled Valentia, and the others giggled and copied her, puffing out clouds of steam.

'Children,' called Balbus, 'keep close. Remember, the dark is not safe. *Night hides earth and heaven . . . and evil schemes.*'

Valentia chuckled. 'Old cowardy-cat,' she said.

But Perry looked anxiously from side to side. What was hiding in those shadows and alleyways? Was this where something awful was going to happen to Valentia – right here, in the street, on the way to school? Maybe there were thieves with daggers or . . .

A snarling dog leapt from a doorway.

'Run!' he yelled, and grabbed Valentia as she stumbled along, trying to gather up her long skirt.

Carotus danced backwards, hooting and making faces at the dog. 'Nyah, nyah, you can't catch us,' he taunted. 'It's chained up, you cuckoos,' he called, turning to run after the others.

'Decorum, Valentia,' chided Balbus, when the three of them hurtled up beside him. 'You are the daughter of an important person.'

Valentia gave a sigh, and the bells on her bracelets tinkled noisily as she shook her long, flowing robe.

'I can't run in this silly thing anyway,' she grumbled. 'Mother said I'm not allowed to wear a sash now. I have to dress like a town girl.'

As they turned into the busy street that led to school, they could smell food cooking in the shops, and see flames flickering in ovens and grills, lighting up the faces of storekeepers and customers. Other lights danced along the road ahead of them. Were they more students heading for school?

The sound of squawking chickens made Perry turn his head.

'We're there,' he cried. 'There's the shop with the hens and rabbits, and the shoe shop ... And there's the staircase,' he added, pointing at a high flight of stone steps.

He felt for the stylus tucked into his belt. Now he'd have a proper use for it!

But when he looked at Valentia he saw her face tighten with nervousness.

'Ah, we'll buy your breakfast here, Valentia,' said Balbus, stopping in front of the pastrycook.

'I don't feel like eating,' mumbled Valentia.

Of course, the old tutor didn't hear her, and a moment later he placed a hot pie in her hands.

It smelt delicious.

'I'll have it if you don't want it,' said Carotus.

He and Perry gazed hopefully at the freshly baked pastry, dotted with crispy specks of honeyed ham. They'd eaten stale bread and dried fig paste for breakfast before Valentia even got out of bed.

But Valentia lifted the pie to her mouth and they watched her teeth crunch into the pastry.

Balbus glanced at the sky. 'The sun's coming up,' he said. 'Make haste.'

'Who cares if I'm late,' Valentia shrugged, but she ate quickly and let the old tutor hustle her towards the staircase.

'Remember ... address the teacher ... as *sir*,' puffed Balbus.

At the top was a doorway covered by a heavy curtain. The children looked at each other. Valentia drew in a deep breath, and Carotus pulled back the curtain.

They had a glimpse of a large room lit by oil lamps, then Valentia stepped inside, and the others crowded in behind her.

Perry looked around. Boys and girls were perched on benches around a young man.

The teacher, thought Perry.

The man was draped in a long, rust-coloured mantle and seated on a raised dais. He looked around as they walked in. He had a humorous face and twinkling brown eyes.

'Greetings, young lady. What is your name?' he enquired.

'Greetings, sir. I am Camilla Valentia.'

'Ah, Camilla – the heroine in Virgil's poem, *Aeneid*,' he exclaimed. 'Well, Camilla Valentia, I invite you to take a seat among your fellow pupils.'

He swept out an arm, grabbed his mantle as it slid from his shoulder, and fixed his eye on a girl sitting in the centre. She looked about ten years old. 'Flora, I am sure you can make room for our new pupil.'

Flora pouted, shifting till there was just enough space beside her.

'But what about . . .' Valentia glanced around at Perry and Carotus, then her voice faltered and she moved silently towards the reluctant Flora.

Perry stared at the teacher and waited. The man didn't seem to notice he and Carotus were there.

'What . . .' Perry started to ask, and felt a warning shove in his back. He spun around.

Carotus was stumping to the side of the room. And then Perry realised that the slaves and tutors were seated along the walls, most of them on the floor.

Balbus lowered his bulk to a small stool, and the boys wriggled in beside him, sitting cross-legged on the hard floor.

'This isn't fair,' Perry whispered. All he could see from here was the teacher's head and the backs of the students on the benches in front of him.

'So now, pupils,' said the teacher, beaming a toothy smile, 'I think we should learn a piece of Virgil's *Aeneid*! Thalassus, find me the scroll.'

By bobbing from side to side, Perry could see a

wooden scroll box at the teacher's feet, and, for the first time, he noticed a man on a cushioned stool by the dais. The man rummaged in the box and straightened up, holding out a rolled-up length of old, yellowy-brown papyrus.

'Here, Ammonius sir,' he said.

The teacher hitched up his slipping mantle and began unrolling it.

'Ah, here is the portion I want you to learn,' he said. 'Listen!'

As Thalassus held up the scroll for him, Ammonius spread his arms wide and declaimed dramatically: '*Besides these comes Camilla, of the Volscian tribe, leading a battleline of women on horseback . . .*'

Perry tried to see Valentia's face. He knew she'd love imagining herself leading a battleline.

'*. . . a warrior-maiden,*' Ammonius continued, '*she never trained her girl's hands to the wool basket or spindle . . .*'

'Warrior-maiden?!' squeaked a girl on the bench in front of Perry.

'Camilla Valentia's a warrior-maiden,' gurgled the next girl along, and they collapsed against each other, giggling.

In moments the whole class began to snicker and Perry wished he could yell at them all to stop.

Ammonius stood up so swiftly his mantle fell

off completely. One of the slaves near Perry darted forward, scooped it from the floor and draped it over the teacher's brown tunic again.

'You will take dictation now,' said the teacher sternly. 'Slaves, bring the writing implements.'

Valentia glanced towards Carotus and Perry.

'Quick,' said Perry. 'Where's the ... Carotus, what are you doing?'

Carotus had been given the writing implements to carry to school, and instead of watching the lesson, he was sitting with the wax tablet open on his lap, and a grin on his face, scribbling.

Perry pulled the tablet and stylus away. The wax was messed up with a large picture of a spider all over it. Oh well. Perry slapped it shut and ran across the room to Valentia.

'Do we just sit there all morning while you do lessons?' he asked.

'I guess so,' she said.

Beside Perry, a slave boy handed a wooden notebook to Flora.

'Here you are, miss,' he said.

But Flora didn't glance at him. She was staring at Valentia.

'I can't believe you let a slave talk to you like that!' she gasped. 'He is really badly trained.'

Valentia blushed and looked flustered.

189

Perry stared back at her. What had he said that was so wrong?

'Is everyone ready?' called the teacher. 'The first words are: *Besides these comes Camilla.*'

Valentia threw open her tablet, rolled her eyes, and began to smooth the wax as fast as she could.

'Look,' squeaked Flora. 'The warrior-maiden's still using wax, like a baby!'

Perry and Valentia looked around the circle of benches. All the other pupils had slaves standing in front of them holding ink pots, and all the other wooden notebooks were filled with pages of something that looked like thick, creamy paper. Everyone else was writing with pen and ink!

'Valentia,' said Ammonius, 'you may use a wax tablet this morning but remember to bring ink and parchment in future. We write with ink in grammar school.'

'Baby,' whispered Flora again, and Perry saw Valentia's chin begin to tremble.

He wished he could just snatch up Flora's pot of ink and pour it over the horrible girl's head.

26
RUFUS

AFTER THE WRITING EXERCISE, AMMONIUS called Valentia to come and read out loud. Perry watched anxiously as she walked to the teacher's side.

But Valentia recited clearly and loudly. '*Besides these comes Camilla . . .*'

'Good reading,' the teacher praised her.

Perry and Carotus nudged each other. Good old Balbus. That was one of his favourite quotes.

Then another student was called up, and Perry realised he would have to sit there listening to every single one of them read out loud. He puffed out his cheeks in annoyance. This was not what he'd expected when they set off for school this morning.

He closed his eyes as the voices droned on, and pictured himself at his school back home. It would be maths class, this time of morning. He'd be working through a sheet of problems, getting that little thrill of satisfaction after he finished each one, and Charlie would be scribbling away beside him, racing him to the end of the page . . .

Perry sighed, and opened his eyes. Would he ever see Charlie again, or Liam, or any of his other friends?

He scanned the circle of benches. One . . . two . . . three . . . there were twenty students in the class, but only four of them were girls: Valentia, Flora, and the two older girls sitting in front of him, who looked about fourteen or fifteen.

At last, 'Rufus, you are the final one,' called the teacher.

A tall boy on the far side of the circle rose to his feet. He had tight curls of sandy-coloured hair, and he wore a loose green tunic with big red circles and diamond shapes at the shoulders and hem. As he strode forward, he caught Valentia's eye and smiled at her. His eyes were a greenish colour – like Bucco's.

'What a bubblehead,' sneered Carotus in Perry's ear.

Perry looked at him in surprise. 'Jealous?' he teased.

And then he realised he felt jealous too. Valentia

was *their* friend. She didn't belong with all these snooty strangers.

When Rufus finished reading and turned back to his seat, there was an expectant rustle around the class.

Ammonius settled his mantle firmly on his shoulder, and stepped off the dais.

'Pupils, take a break from lessons and refresh your minds,' he instructed.

Everyone rushed for the door and a moment later Perry was watching in astonishment as they scattered along the footpath, shooting marbles between shoppers' legs, chasing hoops along the paving stones, twirling yo-yos over piled-up shopping baskets, throwing hazelnuts into a cup . . .

'Hey, let's do that,' he cried. 'Bet we can beat them. Come on.' He started to dart forward, but Carotus caught him by the arm.

'We can't play with them,' scoffed Carotus. 'They're not slaves.'

'But . . . we play games with Valentia.'

'That was at the villa. We couldn't play with her here.'

'Oh.' Deflated, Perry looked around for Valentia.

She was standing by herself, watching the girls. They were huddled together, Flora and the two older girls, crouched on the ground, playing a game.

Between their bent heads, Perry could see hands flicking and the flash of something white flying into the air.

Knucklebones! he thought, remembering the games he'd seen at the Arles museum. There'd been a set for visitors to try – made from real sheep bones – and he'd just managed to catch all five when Melissa had dragged him away.

He stepped closer. Flora was placing the knucklebones in her palm. She flicked them in the air and tried to catch them on the back of her hand. All five bones fell off, clattering to the ground. Perry grinned, and he saw Valentia hiding a smile.

'Can I join in?' asked Valentia.

One of the older girls, the one with very black hair and sweeping black eyebrows, glanced up.

She opened her mouth, as if she was about to offer Valentia a turn, but Flora broke in nastily.

'We don't play with warrior-maidens,' she said. 'Here, Modesta.' And she handed the black-haired girl the knucklebones.

'Hang on, it's my turn,' protested the third girl.

She reached to snatch them away, then her expression changed and she looked past Perry with a simpering smile on her face.

'Oh Rufus,' she called in a coy voice, 'can I have a try of your yo-yo?'

The tall, green-eyed boy went on doing fancy, show-off tricks with his little wooden toy as if he couldn't hear her.

'Go up to him, Justina,' said Modesta, giving the other girl a nudge. 'He can't hear you.'

Justina rose to her feet, and sidled up to Rufus. 'Can I have a turn?' she pleaded.

Rufus shrugged, then stood back, with his hands on his hips, while Justina dropped the yo-yo and tangled up the string.

'I don't know how you do it,' she murmured, gazing at him with big eyes. 'You're so clever.'

'You're a clumsy idiot, Justina,' giggled Modesta.

Rufus took his yo-yo back, untangled it, and wound the string again. Then he turned, and held it out to Valentia.

'Do you want a go?' he asked.

Valentia's face broke into a beaming smile.

'Oh, *she* won't be able to do it!' exclaimed Justina.

'No, she's a warrior-maiden,' said Flora.

'A warrior-maiden is more likely to be able to do it than anyone else,' Rufus contradicted her.

'Bubblehead, foot-licker, water-snake,' muttered Carotus in Perry's ear.

Valentia held the yo-yo carefully, and flicked her wrist. The round wooden toy went spinning towards the ground, then hung there, twirling on the end of its string.

The other three girls burst out laughing.

'You just need practice,' said Rufus, winding the string for her. 'We'll do it together.'

Perry gritted his teeth as the tall, confident boy placed his fingers around Valentia's wrist. 'Let go when I say so,' he instructed.

This time the yo-yo climbed halfway up the string again.

'You see, you nearly did it!' he cried.

Perry glanced at Carotus, and they were both glad when Ammonius called them all back to the classroom. The school day finished at lunchtime. Not much longer to go.

'Last lesson will be Greek,' announced Ammonius.

Greek?! Perry glanced at Valentia. Did she know any Greek?

Ammonius gestured at a section of white-painted wall. Someone had written words on it in red ink, in a strange alphabet.

'You will all copy out these lines from Homer's *Iliad*,' said the teacher.

Perry watched Valentia smooth her wax and begin to write, a look of worry and concentration on her face. She wasn't used to doing proper lessons.

He sighed. *These lessons are even more boring than the ones Balbus gave,* he thought.

He glanced at Balbus. The old tutor was asleep, snoring on his stool.

Finally, Ammonius stretched and yawned, adjusting his mantle for the last time.

'All right, you are dismissed,' he said. 'Come, Thalassus.' And the two teachers strode out of the room.

The students shoved their notebooks and pens at the slaves holding their inkpots, and dashed after them.

Valentia, though, didn't have a slave standing in front of her with an inkpot. She had to wait while Perry and Carotus fought their way through the crush to take her wax tablet and stylus for her.

When the two of them reached the bench, they saw Flora was still there too, watching them all with a smirk on her face. She turned, raised her eyebrows at the snoring Balbus, gave a hard stare at Valentia, Perry and Carotus, standing together, then swanned towards the door, her slaves all trailing behind her.

'Balbus, don't be lazy. Wake up!' said Valentia sharply. She thrust her writing things into the boys' hands.

'Walk behind me,' she whispered.

Balbus stumbled to his feet, looking hurt, and drew back the curtain. Valentia stalked straight past him, but as they all fell in silently behind her, Perry thought how lonely she looked, plodding by herself down the stairs in front of them.

27

HAPPY BIRTHDAY

'ARE THEY READY YET?' asked Perry, peering anxiously at the pot of boiling sheep's trotters on the stovetop.

The cook sighed. 'How did I let you boys talk me into this?' she grumbled. 'I've got all the birthday feast to prepare!'

'Yes, but you love us soooo much,' grinned Carotus.

'Get away with you, you cheeky puppy,' said the cook, giving him a good-natured shove.

'It's not really for us,' explained Perry. 'It's for Valentia, for her birthday present.'

The cook poked the steaming mixture with her stirring rod. 'That'll do,' she grunted. She ladled the trotters out of the boiling liquid and slopped them onto a clay dish. 'Mind you don't burn yourselves!' she warned.

The boys rushed the dish to one end of the kitchen table and began to hack at the hot, slippery contents with Carotus's little folding knife.

'Oof, ouch, they're hot,' they laughed, shaking their fingers.

They finally managed to break off the knuckle-bones, and, with lots of blowing, dropping and giggling, they sucked them clean.

'Valentia is going to love our present,' said Perry. 'Your mother made a bag, didn't she?'

'Yes, here it is.'

Carotus untied a little red pouch from his belt and held it out.

'Boys, get out from under my feet,' ordered the cook, and Perry jumped as she slammed a huge dead goose on the middle of the table.

At that moment, Mule-face appeared in the doorway. 'Peregrinus, Carotus, you're supposed to be putting out the silverware,' he rasped.

Hastily, Perry loosened the drawstring in the bag, Carotus filled it with knucklebones, and the two of them scuttled out of the kitchen.

'Valentia!' cried Perry, pulling up short.

The birthday girl was coming down the stairs, wearing a fancy white robe decorated with strips of red. She grinned at the sight of them.

'Isn't it lucky we don't have to go to school

today?' she said. 'I'm so glad it's a market day. I can have my birthday feast right on my birthday.'

Bucco slid from her grasp and she jumped down the last two steps.

'Look what Mother and Father gave me!'

She flung up her arms, jingling the bracelets on her wrists, and fingered the necklace at her throat.

Perry looked at the silver moon hanging from a string of little glass beads. But, mostly, he looked at her large, sparkling eyes.

'You look like an empress!' he said

'You don't look like you,' complained Carotus.

Valentia began to giggle. 'The dress is a bit whiffy,' she confided. 'Habita said the dyers use some sort of stinky stuff to make it so white. Anyway ...' She scooped up her kitten and began to prance down the corridor to the entertaining rooms. 'Mother's invited three ladies to come to the feast, and one of them is bringing her daughter, who's a bit younger than me, and we're going to have all sorts of fancy food to eat just like a real banquet ...'

'Give her the present,' growled Carotus as they hurried after her.

'Present?' Valentia spun round, looking excited.

'Yes, we've got a present for you too,' said Perry, thrusting it towards her. 'I think you'll like it!'

They had reached the fountain in the middle of

the house and Valentia set Bucco on the marble rim. As he peered over, dabbing the water, she seized the bag, shook it and squeezed it.

'Shells?' she guessed. 'Pebbles? No . . . I know!' She wrenched it open. 'Knucklebones!'

'I can teach you how to use them,' said Perry.

Carotus burst in eagerly. 'So you can practise, and get so good at it, you'll impress everyone at that stupid school,' he said.

'But . . .' Valentia's face fell.

Perry knew what she was thinking. 'The others will play with you,' he assured her. 'At my school, when one of the boys brings a new ball, everyone always wants to have a go.'

'As soon as the guests leave, we'll start practising,' promised Valentia.

But now the boys had to help get ready for the party. Slaves were bustling past them, carrying basket-weave chairs with high, rounded backs into the grand reception room next to the dining room.

'Oh, look who's arrived,' said Secundus sarcastically, as Perry and Carotus hurried into the room. 'The corn-heads have decided to come and help.'

Secundus, Vibius and Arro were arranging the seating around funny low tables with bowed legs shaped like animal legs with paws.

'Put those on the chairs,' said Vibius, showing

Perry a stack of red fringed cushions on the floor. 'That is, if you know what chairs are,' he sniggered.

I guess this isn't the kind of banquet where people recline on couches, thought Perry as he bent to pick up a cushion.

The next instant, he felt Carotus snatching the cushion out of his hands and throwing it on the floor. 'Those peacock-feathers can do that themselves,' he growled. 'We were told to put out the silver, weren't we, Apronia?'

He turned expectantly to the housekeeper waiting with a big iron key near the locked silver cabinet. She nodded. 'You did a fine polishing job, too,' she said.

Turning the key in the lock, she lifted out the sparkling washing bowl and offering dish.

'These go on the side table,' she said.

The side table was so tall, Perry had to reach above his shoulders to lay the dishes on its marble top. When he turned back, Carotus was holding a bunch of spoons in each hand, looking puzzled.

'What do you reckon these are for?' he muttered.

'For eating!' Perry eyed them in delight. 'We use them in my time too,' he whispered.

Carotus gave him a funny look. 'That's stupid,' he said. 'What's wrong with fingers?'

Perry thought of how messy it had been at the

villa, eating everything, even the mushiest food, with fingers. 'Er, spoons are neater,' he murmured.

At that moment the mistress swept through the door. She was dressed grandly for the party and Perry stared at the white powder on her face and her pink-painted cheeks. Hadn't that book said the Roman make-up was poisonous? He glanced at Valentia, dancing in, followed by Habita, and blew a sigh of relief. At least Valentia hadn't put on any make-up.

'Sit down, daughter,' said Donata, settling herself near the door.

Valentia dropped on a chair, cuddling her kitten, just as they heard the doorman greeting the first guest. The next moment Vibius was showing a lady, with a group of slaves, into the room.

'Dearest Eugenia,' cried the mistress, rising to her feet and kissing the guest on her cheek.

Eugenia's hair was dyed an unnatural yellow and covered with a red hair net, and her dress was deep red with gold embroidered panels.

Eugenia turned to Valentia, who had risen too. 'This must be the birthday girl,' she cooed.

One of Eugenia's slaves stepped forward and handed Valentia a tiny basket woven from multi-coloured strands. Valentia dropped Bucco to the floor and quickly opened the lid.

'Earrings!' she exclaimed.

She glanced at her mother.

Donata smiled graciously. 'Daughter, next time we go to the baths, we will get your ears pierced,' she said.

The second guest brought a gift of a book – not a scroll or something made of wood, but a real book with a red leather cover and papery-looking pages. Valentia didn't seem very impressed, though. She just laid it on a table, and sat down again, watching the door.

At her feet, Bucco started playing with a strand of ivy he had tugged off the decorations on the tables. He looked very funny, batting it away, then pouncing on it, but Valentia didn't even notice. Perry knew she was waiting impatiently for the girl her own age to arrive.

At last, over the noise of the ladies' chatter, they heard the doorman letting in the final guests.

'My Pomponia, are you well?' cried the mistress, holding out her arms in welcome.

A tall, haughty lady strutted into the room. She had hair dyed bright red, and a huge spray of coloured stones like a collar around her neck. But Perry's eyes sought out the girl walking behind her.

He almost fell over in shock. It was that horrible Flora girl from school!

He glanced at Valentia. She was staring, with

her mouth open. Flora stopped too, looking just as astonished.

Then a yowl sounded from the floor.

Both the girls looked down. Bucco was tugging at his ivy strand, caught under Flora's pink, pearl-trimmed slipper.

'A kitten!' squeaked Flora.

At that instant, the ivy broke in half, and Bucco flipped backwards, somersaulting across the floor.

Flora burst out laughing. 'He is so cute!' she exclaimed.

'He's mine,' said Valentia, picking him up. 'Do you want a hold?' she offered.

Flora's eyes lit up and she held out her arms.

'Flora, remember the presents we brought,' said Pomponia.

'Oh yes!' Flora turned as her mother's slaves stepped forward with the gifts.

From Pomponia, there was a necklace of amber and blue beads, which Valentia immediately dropped over her head, and then . . .

'You'll never guess what I'm giving you,' said Flora with a huge grin. 'It's perfect, and I didn't even know it was you!'

The next slave offered something round, made of dark, glossy wood. Valentia looked puzzled, but as she held out her hand to take it, they all spotted the string dangling down.

'A yo-yo!' she exclaimed.

'I know someone who'll be happy to show you how to use it,' said Flora in a teasing voice, and both girls broke into giggles.

'Our knucklebones are better,' Carotus whispered to Perry.

'And now, Valentia, it is time to make your offering to your guardian spirit,' said Donata. 'Habita, where is her wreath?'

The nursemaid stepped forward with a ring of ivy and parsley and placed it on Valentia's head, taking care not to mess up her fancy hairdo.

'Quick, grab the washing stuff,' hissed Carotus as Arro, Vibius and Secundus headed for the side table.

Perry spun round to grab the jug of water and washbowl. Carotus snatched up the towel. They grinned cockily at the others.

The shrine stood just outside the door. It was shaped like a small temple with the little silver statues standing around a dish of burning embers in the centre.

Perry was used to the ceremony now, but today was special because Valentia was the one making the offering. She beamed as she draped her mantle over her head and washed her hands in the bowl Perry held out for her. Then her face grew solemn as she pinched up a tiny ball of incense and dropped it on the flames. With the perfumed smoke drifting around her, she trickled on some wine, and placed an offering of cake at the feet of a little silver lady dressed in a long mantle and crown and holding a tiny sceptre.

Her voice trembled as she began to pray. 'Guardian spirit, who watches over me and protects me . . .'

Huh, thought Perry. I'm *the one protecting you!*

'In offering this cake, wine and incense,' Valentia went on, 'I humbly pray that you will keep me safe and give me many more birthdays.'

Perry clenched his jaws together.

That little statue can't keep you safe, he thought. *It's up to me.*

He watched Valentia dance back to the party room, laughing, chatting with Flora, scooping up Bucco . . .

She had no idea of the danger she was in.

But I'm going to save you! he promised.

The meal began. There was the huge goose, stuffed with prunes and covered with a sauce of pepper, caraway, garlic, onions and honey. There were boiled parsnip sausages, calves' brain pudding, peas in black cuttlefish ink, and fried snails – eaten, very strangely, using the pointed handles of the spoons.

After that, desserts were carried in on another set of tables: fried dumpling balls with honey and poppyseed, pears brought from the villa, stewed in pepper, cumin, honey, raisin wine and olive oil, and a custard topped with toasted and crushed walnuts, and dotted with black pepper.

Valentia and Flora sat together, leaning close, laughing and chatting as if they were best friends. Flora held Bucco on her lap, running her fingers through his gingery fur, and giggling when he snatched bites off her plate.

The meal seemed to go on forever, but finally the guests rose to leave.

'Now we can play knucklebones,' whispered Carotus, as Valentia moved to the door to bid goodbye to each of the elegant ladies.

The last to reach the door were Pomponia and Flora. The girls looked at each other, then at their mothers.

'Can Flora stay longer, and practise yo-yo with me?' asked Valentia.

'Oh no,' groaned Carotus under his breath. 'Don't let her.'

But a minute later the two girls were shrieking with laughter, the yo-yo dangling and swaying from their fingers, while Bucco tried to bat it with his paws

Back at the villa we could have joined in, thought Perry. *But not here – at least, not with Flora around.*

He glanced at Carotus standing, scowling, beside him.

'At least she's made friends with Flora,' said Perry, tentatively. 'School won't be so horrible for her now.'

But still, it would have been fun to join in.

'Who wants to play with a stupid yo-yo?' growled Carotus. 'She said she'd play knucklebones with us after the party. And she's not. Come on.'

He turned and led the way out of the room. Perry glanced back. Maybe Valentia would call them to join in ... but only Pomponia's slave, lounging around waiting for Flora, noticed they were leaving. Valentia didn't even see them go. He sighed and followed Carotus out the door.

The bag of knucklebones was lying, forgotten, on the floor near the pond. Carotus glared at it then gave it a kick that sent it shooting across the room.

'Hey, don't do that,' said Perry. 'Valentia will play with us another time.'

He ran to pick up the bag, and laid it carefully on the edge of the pond.

'No she won't,' snorted Carotus. 'Valentia's only interested in her posh new city friends now.'

28

THE PAINTED TREE

NEXT MORNING, IT SEEMED THAT Carotus was right. The two boys were waiting by the fountain when Valentia came hurtling down the corridor towards them.

'Quick,' she called, 'I'm meeting Flora. We're walking to school together.'

'See,' growled Carotus.

And after school, when they arrived home, the house was in uproar. There was no more thought of playing games. The doors to the grand dining room were wide open, and strewn everywhere – all over the pretty mosaic floor and spilling out into the hall around the pond – were buckets and jars, trowels and planks of wood, and a swarm of men and boys in dirty, spattered tunics.

Urbinus stood in the midst of it, his long face even longer than usual.

'What's happening?' gasped Carotus.

Valentia beamed. 'Father said he was having the walls redecorated. They must be starting.'

The three of them edged forward, weaving among the workers, to peer into the dining room.

'What a mess!' cried Carotus with glee.

Holes had been gouged in the walls, bars shoved in, and planks balanced across for scaffolding. And men and boys were everywhere, scrambling all over the scaffold with pots and tools, plaster and paint . . .

'Wish we could have a go,' said Carotus. 'That looks fun.'

A tall man teetering on the highest plank slathered the top of a wall with plaster while white lumps plopped from his trowel to the sacking on the floor below. Next to him, a boy with a mop of black hair frantically coloured the damp plaster, dipping a long-handled brush in a little pot of red paint.

'Watch out!' Perry heard him shout, but too late.

The plasterer had knocked the clay pot with his boot and it was somersaulting down, splattering red paint everywhere.

'Idiot, bonehead, sheep's brain,' bellowed the plasterer. 'You should have been holding onto it!'

The boy leaned over the side of the plank with a look of delight on his face. He caught the children's eyes and grinned at them.

Unfortunately, another person noticed them too. 'Carotus, Peregrinus, what are you doing here?' roared Urbinus. 'This is no place . . .'

At that moment, with a flash of ginger fur, Bucco bounded into the room and began to lap at the spilled red paint.

'No, you greedy thing, that's not food!' exclaimed Valentia. 'Quick, Peregrinus, pick him up. He's getting all covered in paint.'

Laughing, Perry bent over to grab the kitten.

'Now take him and get him clean,' ordered Valentia.

Perry glanced at her. Was he just imagining it, or was Valentia sounding even more bossy than usual? He marched off, holding the struggling Bucco at arm's length.

The next afternoon, Perry and Carotus were in the kitchen, attempting to make pizza with no tomatoes, when the black-haired boy appeared in the doorway. He had a green paint smudge on one cheek and a big clay jug in his hands. He grinned at them and held out the jug.

'We've run out of drink,' he said. Then his eyes lit on a pan of chickpeas simmering on the stovetop. 'Could we have something to eat?' he asked.

The cook laid bread, olives and hot chickpeas on a couple of terracotta dishes.

'I'll help carry,' said Carotus, jumping up.

'Me too,' said Perry.

The boy took the jug, filled now with a mixture of water and wine.

'What's your name?' Carotus asked him as they headed for the dining room.

'Melior.'

Mule-face could only scowl at them as they sauntered past him, waving the plates of food under his nose.

The top strip of the walls was finished and the boys tilted back their heads to gaze at the design of green garlands on the red background.

'Did you paint those?' Carotus asked Melior.

'Only the background,' said Melior. 'I haven't learnt how to do garlands yet. I'm still an apprentice.'

'Melior, hurry up here, I need you,' called a young man balanced on the scaffold.

'Coming, Felicissimus.'

Scrambling like a monkey, Melior flew up a rickety ladder and took his place on the plank beside Felicissimus. The young man stretched up his hand to hold one end of a string against the wall.

'Grab it when it stops swinging,' he instructed. 'You know what to do.'

Melior crouched down and Perry saw there was a weight tied to the string. Melior waited till it hung straight then carefully pushed the lower end against the wall.

'Ready,' he said.

'Right, hold tight.'

Felicissimus pinched the string with his free hand, pulled it away from the wall, then let it twang back.

When he rolled up the string, there, running down the wall, was a straight line marked in the damp plaster.

Cool, thought Perry.

Heading home from school the next afternoon, he tried to tell Valentia what they'd seen.

'The string had a weight on it so it hung straight,' he explained, 'and . . .'

'*Ecce*, I forgot to show you I got my ears pierced yesterday!' cried Valentia. 'Look! And after lunch today . . .'

As she babbled on, it was hard to believe this was the same girl who'd squished grapes in the treading pit with them, and learnt to play football in the courtyard. Here, in town, it seemed all she was interested in were new clothes, choosing jewellery, trips to the bathhouse and visits to new, fancy friends.

More like Melissa, thought Perry, with a pang.

He glanced sideways at Carotus. His friend was walking along, scuffing his feet, with a scowl on his face.

But as soon as they got inside, Carotus rushed to see what was happening in the dining room. Mule-face wasn't hanging around and they managed to sneak through the door and watch from a corner.

Melior and another boy were carefully painting large green rectangles on the walls to look like frames – *That's what those lines were for,* thought Perry – and a man was painting scenes inside the frames. He'd made a picture of olive trees with silvery leaves and over-sized olives, and one of grape vines loaded with huge purple bunches, and now he was working on a large building with a row of columns, a dolphin fountain, an arbour . . .

'It's Villa Rubia!' exclaimed Carotus.

'Do you think so?' asked Perry.

It didn't look like the villa really, but, if someone described it to you, well . . . he guessed that was what you might draw.

And then he remembered Mum trying to describe the villa to him, all those weeks ago . . .

Suddenly there was a horrible tight feeling in his chest.

Mum must think I'm dead, he thought miserably.

Two days later, the walls were nearly finished. When Perry and Carotus brought in a meal for the painters and plasterers, they found them all down on the floor, kneeling on the sacking, finishing the last strip along the base of the wall.

'Is it just going to be plain black?' Carotus asked Melior.

'No, it's going to be a garden.'

Sure enough, late in the day, plants and trees began to appear along the background.

'They don't look like trees or flowers I've ever seen,' said Carotus, critically. 'Though I think that one in a pot is supposed to be a citron.'

There were a few animals, too – a white goat with curling horns, a long-legged stork . . .

The apprentices were busy mixing colours, and Melior glanced up as Perry and Carotus came over to watch. 'Nearly finished. Last day tomorrow,' he said.

The boy next to him pounded a yellow chalky lump with a mortar and pestle and poured the powder into a large terracotta jar. Melior took a scoop of the yellow, a scoop of red from another jar, and mixed them in a little clay pot with some grey-coloured water from a jug.

'Here,' he said, adding a paintbrush and handing it to a man wearing a long, fringed cloak.

'That paint's the colour of Bucco's fur,' said Perry. 'And your hair,' he added, nudging Carotus, then ducked, laughing, expecting Carotus to fling round on him angrily.

But Carotus just stared at the orange paint in a strange, intent way. 'Yes, that is the right colour for Bucco's fur,' he muttered.

A few hours later, the painters had put the lids on their paint jars, washed their brushes and left. The doors had been locked, the windows shuttered, and the household gone to bed.

Perry lay on his mat and closed his eyes. He could smell Carotus's stinky bare feet, and the now-familiar scents of smoke and garum floating up from the kitchen below. The room around him filled with the snores of the other slaves.

'Are you awake?' whispered Carotus.

'Mm,' grunted Perry.

Stealthily, Carotus rose to his feet, picked up an oil lamp from a small table, and fiddled with it till the flame burned brighter. Perry still hadn't mastered the trick of doing that.

'Come on,' said Carotus.

'W . . . what are we doing? Where are we going?'

'To paint Bucco.'

'What?'

Perry stumbled after the little, flickering light as Carotus led the way along the corridor, past the curled-up form of Bonica, sleeping outside the door of her mistress, and down the stairs.

Lamps hung on tall stands around the pond, glowing in little pools of light.

But the dining room was in darkness.

'Here, hold it for me,' said Carotus, stepping inside and thrusting the lamp into Perry's hand, 'so I can see what I'm doing.'

The slave boy stooped over, tiptoeing around in the gloom, peering into the little paint pots left lying on the floor.

'This one, I think,' he said, holding one under the lamp. 'Yes!'

It was the orange paint. The Bucco-coloured paint.

Grinning, Carotus picked up a small brush, then knelt down in front of a painted tree. It was the tree he'd said looked like a citron.

'Here comes Bucco,' he declared. 'Hold the lamp close.'

Squatting down, Perry watched him dip in the brush and apply a few strokes. As Carotus worked on the tree, Perry ran his eyes over it. There was a short, brown, twisting trunk and a few dabs of green leaves. He felt as if he'd seen a painting like that somewhere before . . .

The shape of a cat emerged behind the tree.

'Just needs some white,' said Carotus, adding the finishing touches. 'And now . . .' He found some yellow and quickly painted a bulging citron on a branch.

'How's that? Now it really looks like our villa. A citron tree, and Bucco.'

He leaned back on his haunches, beaming at his artwork.

But Perry gaped in shock.

'I know that tree,' he croaked. 'The tree with the cat!'

He got shakily to his feet and stared at it. Yes, if some of the paint was flaked away it would be the tree that he'd seen at the hotel in Arles. The painted tree behind the pane of glass.

'I've seen that tree,' he said in a hoarse voice. 'It's still there in the future. In . . . in the inn where I stayed with my family.'

He could almost feel Dad beside him again, looking at the painting. He could hear Dad's chuckling words. 'I think you've got a good imag- ination,' he'd scoffed. 'All I can see are green and brown blobs.'

'See, Dad,' Perry wanted to crow. 'It *is* a tree. A tree with a cat.'

And then, like a bolt of lightning, it struck him: what if the painting could be his gateway to the future? He'd thought he needed the villa to get back . . .

But what if I don't?! he thought. *It was writing Hello in Latin that did it. Not the ruins. If I use the stylus on the painting and write Goodbye, then it could take me back to the hotel! To Dad!*

'Carotus,' he cried. 'I know how to get back to my own time, to my family! I just need . . .'

With the flame in his lamp flickering wildly, Perry charged back up the stairs.

'What's going on?' panted Carotus behind him.

Perry reached the sleeping room, leapt over the snoring forms sprawled over the floor, and wrenched open the lid of their chest.

Plunging in his hands, he felt frantically through the soft pile of clothes. His fingers closed on something hard . . . no, that was the bath tools. And then he found it.

Leaping to his feet again, he waved the stylus at Carotus, and broke into an excited whisper.

'If I write on your painting . . . *near* your painting,' he corrected, seeing the horror on his friend's face, 'then I can go back to my time.'

He spun towards the door, and then stopped.

I can't go yet! he remembered. *I still have to stay here and save Valentia!*

As Carotus pulled up his cover and fell asleep, Perry huddled on his own mat and tried to think. Valentia would be eleven years, two months and one day old on the fourteenth of January. That was eight weeks away. Was there any chance Mum, Dad and Melissa would still be here waiting in the hotel for him in two months' time?

But even if they aren't, he tried to assure himself, *even if they've gone home, the stylus can take me to the future. It'll be all right. I'll explain to the people in the hotel, say who I am, and I'll get back to Australia.*

Bursting with excitement now, he began to plan ... The very morning he knew Valentia was safe, he would creep into the dining room with his stylus and scratch into the paint ...

He imagined the faces of the people at Hôtel d'Arles when he suddenly appeared out of the wall, and as he lay down, he chuckled softly into the darkness. A warm glow spread over him as he imagined his family laughing and crying back home in Australia when he rang them from the hotel phone ...

29

WHO DID IT?

THE NEXT THING PERRY KNEW, Carotus was shaking him awake.

'Come on, let's have another look at my picture before the painters get here,' he said.

As they hurried past the pond, they skidded to a halt and stared in surprise. By the light of the oil lamps they could see little drops falling from the hole in the roof to the pond below.

'It's rain! It's raining inside the house,' exclaimed Carotus.

Then Valentia appeared, and they all stood together like old times, pointing and laughing, till Balbus hustled them off to school.

'I didn't get a chance to check my picture again,'

Carotus complained in a whisper. 'I hope they don't paint over it.'

'They don't,' Perry assured him. 'I told you, it's still there in the future. It's the only bit of wall that's left!'

That day, after school, Donata met Valentia in the sedan chair, as she often did now, and the boys and Balbus were left to go home alone.

As they headed towards the dining room, they came across Melior kneeling on the floor by the pond, washing brushes in a bucket.

'I'm keeping out of the way,' he said, jerking his chin at the dining room. 'Felicissimus is creating a stink, saying someone mucked up his painting of a tree. He blamed me, but I didn't do it, and no one else is admitting it. But the funny thing is, Tadius – he's the head painter – he says it's really good, and he wishes he knew who did it!'

A big grin spread over Carotus's face. 'Is it a picture of a cat?' he asked.

Melior stared at him, then jumped to his feet. '*You* did it?' he gasped. 'Come on, we've got to tell Tadius!'

Perry came too as Melior grabbed Carotus by the sleeve and hauled him through the doorway.

'I found the boy who did it!' he yelled.

The man with the fringed cloak came striding

towards them and eyed Carotus up and down. 'Who are you?' he demanded.

Carotus grinned cockily up at him. 'I'm Carotus, the slave,' he said.

'Hmmm.' Tadius took in a deep, noisy breath and exhaled slowly. 'Well, Carotus the slave, if your master ever allowed it, I would be happy to have you as an apprentice. It's a good life, as this lazybones could tell you . . .' He cuffed Melior playfully on the side of the head. 'And you never know, if you get skilled enough, your master might set you up in a workshop one day like mine did, and give you your freedom, so you could have a fine business like this!'

Then he turned on his heel and strode back to his work.

The three boys looked at each other.

'Holy Jupiter!' breathed Carotus. 'Imagine grinding colours and splashing paint and plaster around all day instead of the boring things we do now. And painting pictures too!'

Perry didn't think this apprentice job sounded much better than polishing silver or the other chores they had to do, but if it meant the chance to be freed instead of staying a slave . . .

'You've got to ask him then!' Perry exclaimed.

'Ask who? What?'

'Maximus, of course, if you can be an apprentice,' said Perry.

Carotus rolled his eyes. 'You really don't get it, do you? He's my master. I can't just front up to him and say, *Eia*, I don't feel like carrying and cleaning for you anymore or looking after your daughter at school. I'd rather go muck around with paints.'

'Oh.' Perry couldn't get used to this slave business. 'Well, maybe you can ask Valentia then,' he suggested.

'*Vah*, Valentia doesn't care about us anymore.'

Perry was silent. It was true, Valentia never seemed to have much time for them anymore, and when she was with her new friends, she ordered Perry and Carotus around – if she spoke to them at all – in the snobby way the others talked to their slaves. But still . . .

He remembered the way she had laughed with them about the rain coming through the roof . . .

'She does still care for us,' he said uncertainly.

The days passed, and Perry tried to settle into the boring routine of the town house. Urbinus haughtily announced that the two boys could begin serving at dinner parties, and Carotus was pleased, but for Perry it was just one more horrible chore to do – washing other people's smelly feet.

Every now and then, when Perry was doing

something he particularly hated, like using the two-hole toilet, and watching the door in fear someone was going to walk in on him, he wondered why he was staying. He could just warn Carotus of the danger Valentia was in, and then leave.

But ... he had an awful feeling the Romans believed in Fate or Destiny or something. Carotus would probably just say whatever happened to Valentia was in the hands of Fate, and he wouldn't do anything to stop it.

And I can't go away not knowing what's happened to her, he thought. *I have to make sure she's safe. Even if she hardly notices me anymore.*

30

SNAILS AND RIDDLES

ON THE DAY DECEMBER DAWNED, Carotus bounced out of bed, sparkling with cheerfulness. 'Only seventeen days till Saturnalia,' he said.

'What's Saturnalia?'

'You'll see. But I know you'll like it,' replied Carotus mysteriously.

Perry picked up a few hints from the other slaves. Saturnalia seemed to be some sort of festival. And a holiday – a holiday that lasted for seven days.

'The best time of the year!' they all said.

'We have a festival in December too,' Perry told Carotus. 'It's called Christmas. We give each other presents, and have a big feast, and hang up decorations . . .'

His voice trailed away as he realised that this year,

if his family thought he was dead, they probably wouldn't have a party. He wished he could tell them not to worry. *Just a few more weeks*, he promised himself.

'We hang up decorations too,' said Carotus. 'Bet our festival is better than yours.'

'Bet it isn't,' retorted Perry.

When I get home, we'll have the biggest party ever! he decided.

As Saturnalia approached, the students at school grew more and more excited.

'Last day of school tomorrow,' they called to each other as they piled out of the classroom on the fifteenth of December.

The next morning, after buying Valentia her breakfast, Balbus turned to the woman with the hens and rabbit stand.

'Ten plump snails,' he said, holding out a few coins.

The woman turned to a basket on her counter, raised the lid and counted out ten snails. 'There you go,' she said, sweeping them into a small sack.

'You carry them, Peregrinus,' said the tutor.

Bewildered, Perry took the sack. What on earth did they want snails at school for? And then, he noticed other animals being carried up the stairs – a bunch of dead pigeons on a wire hoop, a rabbit

dangling by its paws, a hen with a broken neck ...
Some of the slaves were carrying bundles of holly
and ivy, too.

It must be something to do with Saturnalia, he
thought.

Sure enough, when they reached the classroom,
the slaves presented their burdens to Ammonius and
Thalassus, then piled them up in a corner.

'Thank you, my dear pupils, for all your gifts,'
announced Ammonius. And, for the first time, he
turned to address the slaves, who were murmuring
excitedly together against the wall.

'Boys, put up the decorations,' he said.

'Yes!' cried Carotus, bounding forward and
grabbing a handful of greenery. 'Here,' he said,
rushing back to Perry, 'hold the bits while I make
a garland.'

In minutes, garlands of holly and ivy were strung
over the door and windows.

'Now, pupils, it's time to write your riddles,' said
Ammonius. 'Thalassus will help you.'

Perry took up his new role, standing in front of
Valentia with her inkpot, watching as she struggled
to write on the parchment, her pen dropping blobs
of ink everywhere.

Suddenly, Flora let out a shriek and jumped up,
flinging out her arms. Her inkpot sailed out of her

slave's grasp, crashed on the floor, and shot a fountain of ink onto the line of snails sliming their way over Flora's foot.

The class sputtered with laughter, and Perry saw Valentia flash a glance across the room. He followed her gaze. Carotus was sitting with a smirk on his face, and an empty sack lying by his side. He grinned wider when he saw them looking at him.

Perry glanced at Valentia. She was trying very hard not to laugh.

School finished early that day. The students were too noisy and restless to concentrate. But the moment the teacher dismissed them, instead of rushing for the door the way they normally did, they clustered together, handing each other rolled pieces of parchment – the riddles they'd written that morning.

'Yo Saturnalia!' 'Yo Saturnalia!' they wished each other as they handed over their gifts.

Like giving presents at Christmas break-up at home, thought Perry. *Only I don't think my friends would think much of a handwritten riddle for a present!*

He saw Valentia and the other girls exchange riddles, and then Rufus started to walk towards them.

'Ooh, look who's coming,' teased Modesta, nudging Valentia.

Valentia looked flustered as Rufus reached her,

smiled, and handed her a riddle. He didn't hand any to the other girls.

'Bubblehead, bubblehead, bubblehead,' growled Carotus, as he always did.

And then, with more shouts of 'Yo Saturnalia', everyone rushed out of the room.

As usual, Valentia walked with Flora, while Perry, Carotus and Flora's slaves kept a few paces behind. The girls unrolled their riddles, puzzling over them and giggling together.

'Listen to this one,' said Valentia. '*I am full of harmless fire, I am very warm but no one is afraid . . .*'

'It's your funny-looking slave with the red hair,' screeched Flora, turning to point at Carotus. 'His hair is like fire!'

'Oh, it is, too!' agreed Valentia, and the two of them fell against each other, shrieking with laughter.

Carotus's face went almost as red as his hair. 'I hate this place,' he snarled.

Neither of the boys spoke for a few minutes.

And then, 'Last year, at Saturnalia,' muttered Carotus, 'Valentia gave me my folding knife.'

Perry knew how much Carotus loved that knife. Valentia could not have chosen a better present for him. But now . . .

'I bet she doesn't give me a present at all this year,' Carotus added.

Perry was afraid he was right.

But when they stepped inside the house, and Valentia had waved goodbye to Flora, she turned to the boys with a beaming smile.

'Yo Saturnalia,' she exclaimed, handing them each a rolled-up piece of parchment.

'Yo Saturnalia,' Carotus replied, and it looked as if the sun had come out on his face.

He unrolled his parchment and read the words slowly out loud. '*I weave, I don't use a loom or thread, I don't use my hands, my feet do everything, I'm a . . .*'

Carotus stared at it for a minute, then burst into a chuckle. 'A spider!' he yelled, waving the riddle in the air. 'What's yours, Peregrinus?'

Perry quickly opened his own riddle.

'*I have wool filling me which nobody sees. Hands send me, and hands return me through the air.*'

Perry felt warmth spreading inside him. Valentia had chosen the perfect riddle for each of them. When he lifted his eyes, she was watching him, her face shining with anticipation.

'A ball,' he answered, and his voice came out in a husky whisper.

31

SATURNALIA

'VALENTIA, HAND ME AN OYSTER!' demanded Perry, lying back with a smirk on the dining couch.

'Yes, sir,' chuckled Valentia.

'With lots of sauce on it,' added Perry.

He tilted his head back and tried to suck the oyster neatly off the shell, the way Maximus did.

'Augh!' he squawked, bouncing up, sputtering and laughing, with pepper-and-wine sauce dripping down his chin onto his best tunic.

'Wash my hands and clean my face!' he ordered, tossing the shell and waving his sticky fingers in the air.

'No, my turn on the couch!' bellowed Carotus, and Perry found himself being rolled onto the floor as Carotus flopped down in his place.

Perry clambered to his feet, grinning, and pulled up a stool instead. 'You're right, Saturnalia is better than Christmas,' he said.

'I knew you'd like it,' said Carotus.

'Does every house have a crazy party like this, where slaves swap with masters?' asked Perry.

'Of course.'

'Valentia, bring me a spoon,' called Habita, from further along the couch.

'I want my meat cut up!' called Arro.

'Me too!'

'Over here, Valentia.'

The big reception room rang with shouts as all the slaves joined in the fun.

'Wash my hands!' 'Pour my wine!' 'Hand me bread!' 'Wipe the table!'

'Look, I think the master is serving us too,' cried Perry with glee, as Maximus came in the door carrying two jugs.

'*Eia*, over here,' called Carotus, leaping to his feet and grabbing up a fine wineglass. 'My glass needs filling.'

'You can't talk to him like that,' gasped Perry, but, to his astonishment, Maximus calmly strode across to them, leaned over, and poured a stream of wine into Carotus's cup.

'This is the best wine from the vineyards of Villa Rubia,' he announced. He topped up the glass with water from the other jug, then turned to Perry. 'You too?' he asked.

Beaming, Perry picked up another goblet. He didn't really like wine, but he wasn't going to miss out on being served by the master!

As Maximus moved on, answering the rude shouts of the other slaves, Perry and Carotus turned their attention to the food again. The oysters had been replaced by a platter of small roast animals. They were well-cooked and crispy but Perry could make out four legs on each of them, a shrivelled little head, and a stump where a tail had been cut off.

'Yum,' said Carotus, 'stuffed dormice.'

Perry nearly fell off his stool. He'd almost forgotten about the Romans eating mice.

Carotus picked one up and began to munch appreciatively.

'Mmm,' he murmured, spitting the bones on the floor. 'Go on, try one,' he said.

Bravely, Perry picked up the smallest one and took a nibble.

'Not bad!' he said in surprise. The meat was a bit like crispy pork. He took another bite and got a taste of the stuffing.

'Yeugh,' he said, spitting it out. 'It's got garum in it!'

Carotus roared with laughter.

Perry took a gulp of wine to wash away the taste – he was getting used to awful drinks now.

Valentia came staggering in, trying not to drop two more plates of food. Perry started to spring up to help her but Habita pulled him down.

'She is waiting on us today,' said the nursemaid, in a very satisfied voice.

Valentia dumped the plates near them, and Perry looked at the two dishes with interest.

'What's that?' he asked her.

'Boiled eels.'

'What about the other one?'

Valentia poked her finger under the white sauce. 'Looks like peas.'

Perry picked up a little silver spoon. This was the first time he'd used any cutlery in three and a half months. He scooped up a small bite of peas. There were bits of sausage and nuts and honey in there, too, but nothing that tasted too bad. He quickly scoffed down a few more spoonfuls.

Maximus was moving around the room again, distributing coins this time, from a small pouch. As Perry smoothed the coins in his palm, he thought of the blackened lumps he'd seen in the château. These ones were sparkling and new.

Fresh from the new imperial mint, he thought, remembering that Maximus was an official there.

236

Each coin bore the profile of a stern-looking man with a jutting chin, a wreath on his head and the words IMP CONSTANTINVS in raised lettering around the edge. So this was the famous Emperor Constantine.

'What's the master giving us money for?' he asked.

'So we can buy presents,' beamed Carotus.

'Real presents?'

'Yes,' said Carotus eagerly. 'I wonder what Valentia will buy me this year.'

When everyone had their coins, Maximus strode out of the room.

'Let us play King of Saturnalia now!' hiccupped Urbinus, struggling to sit up.

Perry stared at the usually severe Mule-face. His long nose was bright red and he was lolling on a couch waving a wine cup in the air.

Valentia ran to a high side table and lifted down a strange metal tower with a pattern of little holes in the sides. It looked a bit like a kitchen grater, but it jingled when Valentia picked it up. She pulled the platters off one of the small tables, dumped them on the floor and set the tower in the centre. On the side facing Perry, there was a set of tiny steps leading down from the tower with three bells hanging over them.

'What's that?' Perry asked Carotus.

'The dice tower,' Carotus answered happily. 'They must have brought it from the villa. Watch.'

Urbinus lumbered to his feet, took the three dice Valentia held out to him, and dropped them in the top of the tower. There was a loud rattling noise, and the dice shot out the bottom, rolling down the steps, and ringing the bells.

'Two-two-five,' called Valentia.

'Dog throw,' groaned Urbinus.

Balbus was next.

'As Cato says,' he proclaimed, clasping the dice high in his fists,

When fortune smiles, forget not she may frown;
When fortune frowns, be not too much cast down.'

He threw in the dice then bent close, trying to read the numbers.

'Six-four-one,' Valentia told him.

'How do you win?' Perry asked Carotus.

'By throwing the biggest numbers.'

One by one, everyone had a turn. Vibius shouted excitedly when his dice spat out three fives. 'I'm going to be the winner!' he crowed.

'Nooo,' groaned Carotus. 'Don't let him be the king.'

'What happens if you're king?'

'You get to tell everyone else what to do, and you can make them do ANYTHING.'

'Oh no.' Perry and Carotus stared at each other in horror. 'We can't let him win!' said Perry.

But turn after turn, everyone else threw lower numbers than Vibius. He grew more and more cocky and excited and they could see him muttering with his pals, glancing across at Perry and Carotus and sniggering.

Perry and Carotus were the last two players. Perry picked up the dice slowly. They were worn, squashed-shaped lumps of bone with the dots carved into the sides.

He took a deep breath and dropped them in the top of the tower.

'Four . . . five . . . two,' he said mournfully.

It was all up to Carotus now.

'I'm the winner, I'm going to be king!' crowed Vibius.

Carotus screwed up his face in a scowl and hurled in the dice. The bells seemed to jangle louder than any other time and as the dice rolled out, one of them tumbled onto the floor. 'Five-five!' yelled Carotus staring at the two on the table.

'And six!' he, Perry and Valentia all screamed together as they looked at the one fallen onto the floor.

'Cheat!' bellowed Vibius.

But the cheering around the room drowned him out.

'Carotus for king! King Carotus!' everyone yelled.

Two men hoisted the winner on their shoulders and carried him around the room, laughing and pumping his fists. His hair was bright, shining red in the lamplight. Like a crown.

'What do you command, King Carotus?' they asked, coming to a halt in the middle of the room.

He beamed around at them all. Then he pointed at Urbinus.

'Urbinus, hold your hands up like ears and pretend to be a mule,' he ordered.

Everyone roared with laughter. 'Urbinus the mule,' they yelled, and then they clapped and cheered as he good-naturedly pranced around the room, braying and stamping, and waggling his hands like ears.

Everyone else had to be an animal too. Balbus was told to be a pig, Habita was a sheep, and Valentia was a cat – of course.

She crouched down to crawl on all fours, and it was just like old times, having fun together in the villa. She slurped from a bowl on the floor, leapt all over the furniture and pretended to sharpen her claws down the side of a cupboard.

Everyone applauded, Perry and Carotus loudest of all.

'And what will I be?' Perry asked Carotus eagerly.

When Carotus looked back at him, Perry knew

his friend was dying to tell him to be one of those weird Australian animals Perry was always bragging about, but of course he couldn't.

'A monkey,' decided Carotus.

Grinning, Perry bounced up and down, scratching his armpits and making funny noises.

Finally, it was the turn of the blond boys. They'd been standing waiting on the side, very subdued, with worried expressions on their faces. Carotus slid down from his high perch and strode towards them with a smirk.

Perry held his breath.

'You three,' said Carotus, 'are fish. You have to put your faces in the water and blow bubbles. Valentia, fill up the washbowl.'

There was a lot of teasing and hoots as the bowl was carried to the middle of the room and Valentia's eyes were dancing as she filled it to the brim with cold water.

'Go on. You first, Vibius,' commanded the king.

Vibius knelt down and dipped his chin in the water. There were shrill, jeering whistles all around the room.

'Put it in properly, you coward,' yelled someone.

Scowling, Vibius pushed his face right into the water, blew a few bubbles, then raised his head. Water was streaming off his chin.

'Wait, stay on your knees,' ordered Carotus, as Arro and Secundus did the same.

Perry stared at his friend, half scared, half thrilled. What would Carotus dare do to them now?

The king put his hands on his hips and looked at the boys kneeling at his feet. 'Fish need water,' he announced. And, sweeping up the bowl, he poured the remainder of the cold water all over their long blond locks.

Valentia shrieked, Perry gasped, and the next moment Carotus was hoisted into the air again, the room erupting with cheers and laughter.

32

THE MAGICIAN

'RACE YOU TO THE CORNER!' shouted Carotus, taking off without warning.

'Cheat!' yelled Perry.

But even with a head start, Carotus was no match for him. Perry flew along the footpath, his slate-grey cloak streaming out behind.

'You're too fast!' laughed Carotus, coming to a panting halt behind him.

They turned in the direction of the market and Perry pulled his hood back over his head. It had started to rain.

A procession was heading down the middle of the road towards them, musicians leading the way, blaring on trumpets and long wooden whistles.

'Another funeral,' said Perry.

There seemed to be an awful lot of funerals in Arelate. He'd learnt to recognise the noise of the musicians, and the crowd of paid mourners, stumbling along, wailing and tearing their hair out.

'There's the dead person,' cried Carotus, pointing past them.

As usual, the body was not in the coffin yet. It was lying on a wooden couch, decorated with garlands, and rocking and swaying in the air as men carried it along.

Perry didn't like the idea of seeing a dead body, but he couldn't help peeking.

'It's a boy!' he exclaimed, and then, 'It's Lepidus!' they both gasped together, and stared at each other.

'That's why we haven't seen him at school for days,' said Carotus. 'He's dead!'

Perry felt a horrible, hot, sour taste rise up in his throat.

'I wonder what he died of,' said Carotus, as the procession went on past.

Perry gulped, trying desperately not to be sick.

The real mourners had reached them now: a man with a white face, jaw clenched, a woman sobbing, a tall girl with elfin features like Lepidus's, but all red and swollen from crying ...

Perry swung away, scrubbing at his own eyes. In two weeks, if he didn't stop it, Valentia would be lying like that on a couch, with Maximus and Donata walking behind . . .

No! He wouldn't let it happen.

'I'm getting soaked standing here,' said Carotus. 'Come on. *Eia*, what's the matter? Don't you have dead people in your time?'

'Of course we do. But they're not usually children.'

Perry tried to wipe his eyes with the edge of his cloak, but it was too wet.

'Listen . . . I have to tell you another secret,' he said. He couldn't keep it to himself anymore.

'I know,' said Carotus, 'you're not really from the future, you've been making it up all along!'

'No.' Perry gave a wan smile and took a deep breath. 'In the future,' he said, 'I saw Valentia's coffin, and . . . it said she died when she was eleven years, two months and one day old!'

Carotus's eyes grew as round as tennis balls. 'Holy Jupiter!' he exclaimed.

Perry clenched his hands into fists. 'But it's not going to happen,' he declared.

'You just said it's written on her coffin!' protested Carotus.

'I know. But she is not going to die. I'm not going to let it happen.'

'How can you stop it? Are you going to tell her? Warn her?'

'Of course not! Imagine how that would feel! She'd be counting down the days, waiting to die . . .'

A mischievous expression crept over Carotus's face. 'That could be useful,' he said. 'You could do anything you wanted and get away with it by dying!'

'That is not funny,' answered Perry. 'Anyway, she is not going to die. And you are not going to warn her. Promise me you are not going to tell her.'

Carotus shrugged. 'How do you think you are going to save her, then?'

'I don't know. I don't know what's going to happen to her. But I've done . . .' He tried to think how to explain a First Aid course. 'I've learnt ways to save people.'

'You mean magic?!' cried Carotus.

'No, just . . .'

'But that's what we can do!' said Carotus, pointing excitedly towards the market. 'Remember, we saw that man who sells magic spells. We can buy one. We've still got some money from Saturnalia. Come on!'

And Carotus took off, diving through the arch between the shops and disappearing into the noisy, messy market beyond. Perry dashed after him, weaving among shouting sellers, baskets of stinking fish, beggars with clawing hands, and clay pots of smelly pickles, till at last he spotted the magician.

The man was surrounded by a ring of gasping onlookers and Carotus was bouncing up and down on his toes, trying to see past the crowd.

'Come on, let's get to the front,' he said when Perry reached him, and the two of them weaselled their way through.

The magician's costume might have looked all right in summer but now, in the middle of winter, he looked wet and bedraggled. Rain trickled from the top of his shaved head onto his fake-leopard-skin cape, and the painted spots were dissolving in a soggy yellow and brown mess, dripping onto his long white robe.

As the two boys reached the front, the magician uncoiled a snake from a basket. 'Behold this venomous creature,' he trumpeted, 'a creature that can deal death with a single bite!' He leapt forward to swing it around the circle, and everyone jumped back. 'But, heed, my spells protect me,' he cried.

He thrust the head of the snake right inside his mouth and the crowd gasped, then he pulled it out again and waved it in the air.

Perry knew it had to be a trick, but when he glanced sideways, he saw his friend clapping wildly, his face lit up with wonder.

'For a few coins, you too can guard against fear,' the magician warbled, waving his hands at scrolls spread out on a small table. 'What do you dread? Pestilential fever, black bile, dropsy?'

His piercing black eyes scanned the circle and people began to move away, but Carotus leapt forward.

'I want something that protects against everything,' he declared.

'Ah, for that, you need this spell,' said the magician.

He lifted the largest scroll, stroked it reverentially, and unrolled one corner. Perry was startled to see the word 'Abracadabra' written over and over. He would never have guessed that was an ancient Roman spell word!

'How do we use it?' asked Carotus.

'You burn it to ashes, and then you drink it.'

Carotus looked gleefully at Perry. 'We can drop it in her wine!' he said.

'Like a caterpillar,' grinned Perry.

It wouldn't really work, but it might stop Carotus spilling the beans to Valentia.

'And now we need to buy her New Year present,' said Perry.

'And the garlands for the master's banquet,' added Carotus, and they both turned to look around the market.

33

NEW YEAR'S EVE

THE MARKET WAS A GRAND public square. A painted statue of a goddess sat on a throne in the centre, surrounded by elegant soaring columns. And around the sides were the shops, their wares spilling out over the marble paving stones, while the stallholders yelled for customers and waved their goods in the air.

'Fresh fish!'

'Best hares!'

'Five eggs for one *nummus* – don't miss this bargain.'

A butcher slung a pig's head on a hook, dripping blood on the stone floor, a grocer scooped her soggy vegetables from their huge clay jars of smelly, slimy brine, a potter stacked his shiny red bowls on his counter, letting out a yell when one of them fell to the ground and smashed . . .

The customers were mostly men. They haggled with the bellowing stallholders, poked and sniffed at the goods, and ordered their slaves to carry their loaded baskets.

Perry stared around as he followed Carotus from shop to shop.

'Here's a backscratcher,' cried Carotus, 'like Valentia bought me for Saturnalia.' He picked up the long arm made of bone and tried to scratch Perry's head with the tiny hand carved on the end of it.

'If you're not buying that, leave it alone,' said the stallholder.

'What sort of presents are we looking for?' asked Perry.

'Sweet things to eat, for a sweet New Year,' said Carotus.

The honey stall was a milling mass of customers, most of them clamouring for the big clay pots labelled 'Superior honey'. Perry was about to ask for one too, when he realised, miserably, that all he could afford was a tiny pot of ordinary honey.

The shop selling garlands for the New Year banquet was even more crowded.

'Keep close!' yelled Carotus, as he elbowed his way to the counter.

Perry had a glimpse of girls working at a stone bench, while people snatched the garlands they wove as fast as the girls finished them. He caught a scent of pine and bay leaves, and then Carotus was piling swags of dark glossy leaves with midnight blue berries into his arms.

'All right, let's get out of here,' he laughed, and they fought their way out again.

Back at the house, Valentia was playing with Bucco around the fountain.

'She's at home for once,' said Carotus.

'Bucco wants to get in the pond,' Valentia exclaimed when she saw them. 'Are cats supposed to swim?'

'I don't think so,' said Perry, peering through a haze of leaves. 'Here ... I ...' Tentatively, he held out his little honey jar, without letting go of the garlands. 'I got this for you.'

Valentia reached out to take it from his hand.

'Thank you,' she smiled.

'Have a sweet New Year,' he said. *A safe New Year*, he thought anxiously.

'Come on, we've got work to do,' called Carotus.

'This is fun,' said Valentia, coming to join them, Bucco prancing beside her.

The boys dumped their load of garlands on the dining room floor.

'Where's the best place to hang them?' pondered Valentia.

They all gazed around. The room looked very fancy already with the new painted pictures on the walls.

'I think up high,' she decided.

'There's a ladder for us,' said Carotus, and he crossed to the wall to peer up. 'And I can see nails.'

'You climb and I'll hand up the garlands,' suggested Perry, dragging over a stool to stand on.

'Bucco, no,' cried Valentia behind him, and Perry spun round to see the kitten leap onto the pile of leaves.

Perry plucked him away, then eyed the top garland ruefully. Half the berries had been knocked off. Oh well. Hopefully Maximus and his guests wouldn't notice.

'What do you do for New Year in your time?' asked Valentia as Perry hopped onto the stool.

'We have . . .' he paused, trying to think how to explain fireworks. 'We shoot fire into the sky,' he said.

'You mean, like lightning?'

'No, it's all different colours . . .'

'Coloured lightning!' chuckled Carotus.

'No,' Perry protested again. 'It's not lightning, it's . . .' But some things in the future were just too hard to explain.

Shrugging, he lifted the garland high, and Carotus looped one end over a nail, then slithered down to move the ladder.

'Carotus, look,' cried Perry, jumping off the stool and pointing at the bottom of the wall, 'your painting's still here. See, I told you.'

'What do you mean, Carotus's painting?' asked Valentia.

The boys glanced at each other. 'See if you can find it,' said Carotus. 'I sneaked in one night while the painters were here.'

Valentia looked at him in astonishment, then knelt down next to Perry.

'Oh!' she cried. 'It's Bucco! Behind that citron tree.'

'Carotus put the fruit on the tree, too,' said Perry.

Carotus broke into his cheekiest grin. 'Those painters have no idea what real trees, flowers and animals look like!' he snorted.

'You're so clever!' Valentia sprang to her feet again. 'You should have seen the cat Modesta drew the other day. She forgot to give it a tail!'

They all broke into giggles together.

'I bet I could do better than any of those,' boasted Carotus, waving his arm at the other paintings on the walls. 'The head painter said I was good. He said I could be his apprentice, but . . .'

'Valentia, ask your father to let him,' Perry broke in eagerly.

Carotus and Valentia both stared at him.

'You're funny, Peregrinus,' said Valentia. 'Children don't tell their parents what to do, it's the other way around. But look, I haven't given you your present yet!'

She ran to the side table. A row of the most expensive jars from the honey shop stood along the top of it.

For Maximus to give his guests at the banquet tomorrow, thought Perry.

Valentia reached across the jars and pulled out a lamp made of red clay.

'Here! Have a sweet New Year.' She placed it in Carotus's eagerly outstretched hands. 'It's for both of you,' she said. 'Look, it's got a tiger on it. I couldn't find one with a cat.'

Carotus tilted it so Perry could trace his finger over the raised shape of the tiger.

Then Perry felt a nudge in his ribs. Carotus was grinning at him. 'You'll have to work out how to use a lamp now!' he said.

34

EMPEROR CONSTANTINE

'THE IDES OF JANUARY!' CRIED Carotus, leaping off his sleeping mat.

'Oh no,' groaned Perry, sitting up and covering his face with his hands. 'It's tomorrow.'

'What are you talking about? He's coming today! Come on, we don't want to miss a thing.'

'Who . . . what? Who's coming?'

'The emperor, stupid! Where've you been hiding?'

'Oh.'

The city had been busy for days getting ready for a visit from the emperor, but Perry had been too worried about Valentia to pay attention.

'Come on,' said Carotus again, throwing off his everyday tunic and pulling on his new, grand one, made specially for today. 'Here.'

Perry's new tunic was dropped on top of his head.

'Get dressed,' Carotus ordered, 'and stop being such a misery-guts. What's got into you?'

'I'm worried about tomorrow,' said Perry.

'What's tomorrow?' asked Carotus, trying to use the little hand on his backscratcher to pick up his leggings.

Perry glanced around. The only people left in the room were chattering noisily and excitedly. He leaned closer to Carotus. 'Valentia's supposed to die, remember?' he said.

'Oh!' Carotus stood for a moment, staring at him, then he flung down the backscratcher and plunged his arm in the open chest. Next moment he was pulling out the spell scroll they'd bought in the market. '*Ecce*, we'll burn this today, and put it in her wine!' he announced triumphantly.

Moments later, they were tumbling down the stairs and into the kitchen.

'*Eia*, what are you up to now, you monkey?' demanded the cook as Carotus thrust the end of the scroll in the embers of the stove.

'A spell to make a wart grow on your nose,' chortled Carotus.

He pulled out the flaming scroll, dropped it in one of her clay cooking pots, and crouched on the floor with Perry. They watched it burn down to powdery grey cinders.

'Now what?' whispered Perry.

'I'll hide it, and we'll sneak it into her drink later,' beamed Carotus. 'Now come on, grab something to . . .'

They were just reaching for some bread when Urbinus appeared in the doorway, trumpeting for them.

'Carotus, Peregrinus, the master wants you.'

The boys looked at each other, Carotus shoved the ashes behind a huge clay jar of lentils, and they hurried out of the kitchen stuffing the bread in their mouths.

People were everywhere, rushing in and out of rooms and up and down stairs.

'No one wants to miss the arrival,' said Carotus excitedly. 'Emperor Constantine coming to Arelate!'

They reached the door of the master's room and Carotus fell silent. Maximus was seated on a high-backed chair dressed in strange clothes: two long tunics, one on top of the other, and shoes with straps around his ankles. A man hovered at the side of the room, and beside him a couple of strange slave boys were trying to support a huge weight of folded cloth between them.

'Boys,' called Maximus when he saw Perry and Carotus in the doorway, 'pour my drink.'

Perry had to stop himself from rolling his eyes at Carotus. Jugs of water and wine stood right there on a table by Maximus's hand. But his lordliness couldn't pour his own drink. He'd had to send for slaves to come all the way from the kitchen to serve it for him!

Maximus took a few sips, then rose to his feet, gesturing to Perry and Carotus to clear away the table.

'And the chair,' he ordered.

Puzzled, they each took a side of the big chair and heaved it across the room. As soon as the space was cleared, the strange man stepped forward, snapping his fingers for the two slaves with the cloth.

Perry and Carotus stared from the doorway as the strangers began to wind the cloth around Maximus: over his left shoulder, under his armpits . . . a pause to arrange the folds, then around again, over the shoulder, across the front . . .

Perry thought of the American woman in the château, wrapped in her bedsheet. Maybe her costume hadn't been so wrong!

Maximus took the last bit of cloth, looped it over his left arm and turned towards the door.

Perry and Carotus ducked out of sight.

'That's a toga!' whispered Carotus as they dashed away. 'Balbus told us people wore them hundreds of years ago but I thought they were only for statues now.'

'It didn't look very comfortable,' said Perry. 'He'll have to keep his arm up or it will fall down! I wonder why he's wearing it.'

'To look grand, I guess. He's in the greeting party for the emperor at the gate.'

'The sedan chairs are here,' shouted the doorman.

From all over the house people came hurrying towards the front door. Donata and Valentia burst out of a room near the boys. They were draped from head to foot in jewels. Valentia beamed at Perry and Carotus.

'Come on,' she cried.

As they came outside, Maximus was climbing into his sedan chair. A second chair waited behind.

'That one's for us!' said Valentia excitedly.

For a moment, Perry thought she meant he and Carotus should climb in too, but it was Donata who took the other place.

The four bearers hoisted up the chair, and Perry and Carotus ran alongside holding onto the edge while Valentia peeked at them through the curtain.

'Where are we going?' asked Perry.

'The forum, remember? We're meeting the

teachers there so we can hear the emperor give his speech. Mother's coming too, to join the other important ladies.'

Every building they passed was festooned with garlands pinned over doorways and strung between windows. But, 'The street's not as crowded as I thought it'd be,' said Perry.

'Father said everything will be crammed later,' said Valentia. 'That's why we're going early.'

The sedan bearers turned into the market and Perry gazed at the huge, grand staircase leading up to the forum from the far side of the square. He had never been up there before, and now, to reach it, they would have to get through the mob surging around the market. The garland shops were even busier than they'd been on New Year's Eve. Customers filled the whole square, trying to buy wreaths and garlands or fight their way out again.

Perry and Carotus were almost torn from Valentia's side, but they hung on, and at last they were climbing the stairs, the chair rocking and bouncing between the bearers.

At the top of the stairs they came to a halt in a giant entrance porch about two storeys high, with columns soaring upwards to hold up the roof. Through the entrance, Perry could see a vast open space with a stage set up in the middle. *For the emperor's speech,* he thought. A covered walkway surrounded the four sides of the forum. More columns lined the walkway, and behind them Perry could see people beginning to gather. He recognised Ammonius, Flora, and some of the students from school standing in a group.

The bearers lowered the sedan chair and Donata and Valentia clambered out, their jewels sparkling in the sunlight. Valentia was bouncing with excitement.

'We're going to see the emperor!' she said. Then she spotted her schoolfriends, and immediately became more haughty. 'Get behind me,' she told Perry and Carotus.

Donata and Valentia were waved past the guards at the entrance. But the moment Perry and Carotus tried to follow, the guards clashed their spears together, barring their way.

'No scum in here,' growled one of them. 'Take yourselves off. Clear the path.'

'But . . . that isn't fair!' exclaimed Perry.

He waited for Valentia to notice they were missing, to turn and glance back over her shoulder for them. But she didn't. She just kept on walking towards her class.

Carotus's face screwed up in a scowl as Flora, Justina, Modesta and Rufus welcomed Valentia behind the barrier, and the girls all kissed each other on the cheeks.

More people were coming up the stairs now.

'Go on, we told you boys to clear off,' called one of the guards.

'She just forgot all about us,' growled Carotus as they climbed slowly down the stairs again.

But Perry was silent, thinking about the way Melissa acted all grown-up in front of her friends, treating him as if he was just a boring little brother. At home she could muck around and tease him, laugh and complain with him about Mum and Dad . . . But when she was with her friends, he knew, she had to fit in with them.

Like I'm doing here! he realised. He stopped short at the foot of the stairs, ignoring the crowds buffeting around him. *I have to behave like a slave, or . . .*

He grabbed Carotus by the arm. 'Valentia can't help it,' he said. 'She's the daughter of a grand, important person. She has to act the same as the other grand, important people or she won't fit in. You're always telling me slaves have to be quiet, and do what they're told, and all that stuff. Well, it's the same for her.'

For a moment Carotus kept his head down, grinding a few fallen berries under his toe, then he gave them a kick and looked up.

'I suppose so,' he said reluctantly. 'But . . . what are we going to do now? How are we going to see the emperor?'

Perry turned slowly and looked back up the grand stairway.

There were more guards there now, bristling with spears, ferociously examining each person who came up the steps.

And then a movement higher up caught his eye.

'Look,' he gasped.

They both stared at a man edging his way up the red tiles of the walkway roof. He hauled himself onto the ridge, then sat there, gazing down into the forum.

'And there's more of them,' cried Carotus, pointing.

'We can do that too!' said Perry. 'Come on, I'll give you a leg up.'

He was always climbing onto roofs to retrieve balls. This roof was higher than any he'd been on before, but still . . .

In a few minutes, laughing and gasping, he had reached the top, and pulled himself to a sitting position.

'W-o-w,' he breathed out. And then, *I'm glad Mum can't see me up here.*

He was staring down a long, long way to the huge square below, and when he turned his head, he could see the line of road stretching all the way from the main entry to the forum, down through the arched gateway of Arelate, and into the distance.

'We get a better view than Valentia,' crowed Carotus, clambering up beside him. 'We'll be able to see the emperor arriving!'

Other people perched on the roof began to call out and point.

'What are they pointing at?' asked Carotus. 'I can't see anything.'

Perry squinted into the distance. 'I can see . . . something,' he said.

It was about the size of an ant, moving, far, far off on the road. But as he watched, it seemed to turn into a column of ants, coming closer and closer.

And then, 'Soldiers!' they both exclaimed together.

Hundreds of horsemen in fierce-looking helmets were riding down the road. Perry stared at their huge red shields, their dangling swords, their high golden standards swaying in the sunlight. He caught the distant sound of thudding hooves and jingling chains, then it was swallowed up in a wave of noise as the crowds along the route began to cheer.

'There's more!' cried Carotus, pointing excitedly past the horsemen.

The boys watched in awe as the long procession made its way towards the gate.

Behind the horsemen came foot soldiers, and then . . .

'Barbarians,' shouted a man sitting on the roof beside them.

Perry and Carotus gaped at the strange, huge men riding on horses that looked too small for them. They had long blond moustaches, bright blue eyes, and hair shaved on the sides so their faces seemed to bulge.

'They don't look anything like Romans,' said Carotus.

The barbarians were bare-legged with short tunics, hairy rawhide boots, swords slung from their shoulders and long, barbed lances in their hands.

And then, 'There he is!' shouted Carotus, almost falling off the roof. 'The emperor!'

Surrounded by a bodyguard of white-garbed soldiers, and riding on an open cart shining with gold, was Emperor Constantine.

He sat on a throne for all to see, but as his cart drew near the great arched gateway and the roaring crowds, he didn't wave a hand or even turn his head. He might have been a statue.

The procession halted.

'For the greeting party,' said Carotus. 'And the master!'

The cheering died down, and they could hear the sound of chanting from the other side of the wall.

The emperor still didn't move a muscle.

Perry gazed past him at the rest of the procession. It looked like a moving farmyard. There were flocks of sheep, hundreds of pigs, and wagons loaded with hay.

At last the procession began to pour through the archways.

They could see the emperor clearly now.

'He looks just like his portrait on the coin,' said Carotus.

He had a jutting chin, a strong nose, and a stern expression. His long robe was a deep reddish purple, smothered with gold embroidery, and he wore a gleaming, jewelled crown the same shape as the wreath from the coin.

The procession neared the forum, and the boys swung round to look at the groups waiting in the big square below. There were men holding up statues of gods, a band clashing and shrieking on their weird instruments, a group dressed in long white robes who looked like Christian priests ... Perry caught a glimpse of Valentia, leaning forward to peer between the columns, and he felt a jolt of shock as he remembered the danger facing her tomorrow; then she vanished out of sight as the procession came flooding over the courtyard.

There were the grand officials in gold and purple cloaks with bright red belts, there was the emperor's bodyguard in shining white tunics, and there was the emperor himself.

'He's moving!' cried Perry.

Emperor Constantine stepped from his horse-drawn wagon to the dais, raised his right hand, and turned slowly and majestically.

The crowd erupted. Perry could feel the roar pulsing up through the roof, throbbing through his whole body. He turned to grin at Carotus and saw the slave boy – and everyone else on the roof – joining in the chant.

'Augustus Constantine,' they roared. 'Augustus Constantine!' And then, 'May the gods preserve you!'

Wish Mum could see this! thought Perry, his heart pounding with excitement.

Then the emperor seated himself on an elaborate stool in the centre of the dais, and as the cries died away, Perry saw an official in front of the crowd, waving his arms and giving a speech.

'The entire city speaks with one voice and gives thanks to you, most sacred emperor, as a benefactor . . .'

As the pompous words droned on, Perry leaned from side to side, trying to catch another glimpse of Valentia.

The long speech came to an end at last.

'Is Constantine going to talk now?' asked Perry.

But the emperor remained seated, and another official launched into an even more flowery oration.

Perry sighed and turned to gaze around. From up here, he had a view of nearly the whole town. The huge crowds that had blocked the main thoroughfare were moving away. He could see people, soldiers, sheep and pigs wandering along the side roads.

When the next official pushed forward to give a speech, he turned to nudge Carotus.

'Let's go,' he said. 'This is getting boring.'

But the slave boy had managed to scrape some lichen off the roof tiles, and he was sliding chunks down the slope, his eyes lit up with mischief.

As Perry watched, a man in a long white robe touched his hand to his bald head, then lifted an angry face to look upwards. Carotus met Perry's eyes with a grin.

'I think it's time to go,' he said.

They began to scramble down the roof.

'If we get home before the others,' said Carotus, dropping to the ground, 'we can work out how to hide that spell in Valentia's wine. Come on!'

And the two of them raced out of the deserted market, heading for home.

35

THE PLAN
GOES WRONG

'GODS AND GODDESSES, WHAT ARE you doing here?'

Perry was jerked awake by a toe kicking him in the ribs. His eyes flew open and he looked up into the broad face of Habita, looming over him from the open door of Valentia's bedroom.

'What are you doing here?' she repeated. 'I nearly tripped over you.'

'Is Valentia all right?' he cried, sitting up on his mat.

'Valentia? Of course she is. She's sound asleep.'

'No I'm not,' murmured a sleepy voice, and Perry thrust his head round the door to see a familiar figure stretching out in bed, giving a loud yawn. A little, whiskery kitten face popped up beside her. 'What are you doing there, Peregrinus?' called Valentia.

'Just making sure you're safe,' he replied.

She burst into giggles. 'You are so funny! What could happen to me while I'm sleeping?'

He tried to smile back, but he couldn't. Anything could have happened. A snake could have crept in and bitten her, the ceiling might have fallen on her head . . . But Valentia had no idea that today she was supposed to die, and that he was going to rescue her.

'Get up, and move out of the way,' grunted Habita, 'unless you want to empty the piss-pot.'

Perry jumped hastily aside as the slave called Gluppus pushed his way in. Gluppus had the revolting job of collecting all the toilet pots from the bedrooms each morning.

But Perry stayed there, hovering around, waiting for Valentia.

When she came out, carrying Bucco in her arms, she was dressed in one of her grandest new outfits. She even had sparkly silver pins holding up the plaits on top of her head.

'We're not going to school today,' she announced merrily. 'Father says he's taking me to see the mint.'

Perry stared at her in dismay. Why did Maximus have to pick today, of all days, to take his daughter gallivanting around town?

I had it all planned out, he thought. *The safest route to take down the dark streets to school, an extra lamp to light up the shadows, but now . . .*

'Come and serve me breakfast,' said Valentia, heading down the corridor.

'But, uh . . . you don't look very well,' he improvised, running after her. 'I think you should stay in bed all day.'

She turned around, laughing. 'Don't be silly. I'm perfectly well. And I'm certainly not going to miss out on going to the mint!'

As she descended the stairs, he closed in behind her, stretching out his hand to catch her if she fell. He was so close, he trod on her long skirt.

'Watch it,' she warned, 'you nearly tripped me up.'

Perry felt hot all over. That was no way to keep her safe!

He breathed a sigh when they reached the bottom of the stairs.

'I think I'll eat here this morning,' said Valentia, turning into one of the rooms off the corridor.

A kitchen slave carried in the food, and Perry peered anxiously at the bread and honey . . . surely those couldn't be poisonous.

Carotus appeared in the doorway. 'Everything all right in here?' he asked.

He waltzed inside, smirking, and gave Perry a nudge.

Valentia sent him a suspicious glance.

'Father's taking me to the mint today,' she said. 'And you two are coming with us.'

'Yes!' gasped Perry. This was his chance to stay by Valentia's side, protecting her.

Outside, Maximus and Valentia climbed into a sedan chair and set off through the streets. The buildings were still garlanded for the emperor, and the city was full of excited crowds. The curtain of the sedan chair tweaked open, and Valentia peeked out, her eyes sparkling with excitement.

The three children stared at Constantine's soldiers wandering around in their long brown cloaks and white tunics, and the fierce-looking barbarians with their shaved heads.

'Aren't the barbarians supposed to be your enemies?' Perry asked.

'I think some of them fight for us now,' said Carotus.

Perry looked nervously at these tall men with swords at their hips and barbed lances in their hands. What if one of them decided to start attacking everyone?

He glanced at the sedan chair but the curtain was closed now. His hand reached up to clutch the edge of the chair.

But there's not much I could do against a man with a sword! he thought.

As they turned towards the river, they found themselves caught in a turmoil of people heading to and from the docks. Carotus was dancing with excitement, but Perry fought to hang onto the sedan chair, looking anxiously at the teetering piles of amphorae, wood and stone being hauled past on overloaded carts.

From the corner of his eye, he saw old Balbus struggling to keep up, being buffeted and jostled by the crowds.

Sorry, Balbus, I can't do anything to help, thought Perry. *I have to guard Valentia!*

A huge archway loomed in front of them, leading to the bridge over the river. And the next moment, there was wood clattering under their feet, and they were on the bridge. Perry stared around in astonishment. It wasn't a solid bridge. It was made from planks laid across a long line of boats; the prows formed a strange balustrade along the side, bobbing up and down with the flow of the river . . .

A huge, wide, murky river. Could Valentia swim?

It's all right, he told himself. *She's safe inside the sedan chair.*

They were nearly at the end of the bridge now. He could see the crowd of ships and boats vying for space at the docks on the opposite bank.

And then there were shouts, people in front

crashing into each other, the sedan chair shuddering to a halt. The next moment everyone on the bridge was standing, waiting for something.

'What's going on?' demanded Perry.

Valentia's face appeared between the curtains. 'Isn't this fun?' she said. 'Father says we're lucky to see the bridge opening.'

Perry realised the last part of the bridge was being lifted into the air, like a drawbridge. He could hear the clanking of the chains as it was hoisted upwards. A wooden boat glided towards the opening, then disappeared from sight behind the crowd ahead. Valentia leaned out further, trying to see.

'Careful, don't fall,' warned Perry, pressing close.

'Peregrinus, you're in such a funny mood today,' she giggled.

She turned to look at the other vessels in the docks. To one side, long, narrow boats bobbed on the water, and on the other side there were tubby wooden sailing ships with cobwebs of lines and masts.

'Look at those huge ships!' said Valentia.

Huge?! They're tiny! thought Perry.

Behind them, Balbus warbled one of his recitations. 'As the great Seneca wrote: *To the man who does not know what port he seeks, no wind is favourable.*'

The drawbridge began to lower again, and everyone cheered, pushing forward.

Perry heaved a sigh as they stepped onto dry land.

But his relief didn't last long.

All around them, the loads from the boats were being hoisted up by wooden cranes, and swung around on ropes. The sedan chair had to pick its way past a team of men hauling blocks of marble up the hill with ropes and sleighs.

There was a *crash* from behind and Perry spun round, trying to throw himself protectively against the side of the chair. It kept on moving, and he fell on the ground, staring up at the astonished faces of the bearers, jogging past.

He sat up, rubbing his back.

A giant amphora was shattered on the ground in a pool of wine.

'Felt like a drink, did you?' quipped Carotus, pulling him to his feet.

'No, I . . . Quick, they're getting out!'

The sedan bearers had lowered the chair in front of a plain, squat building, and Maximus and Valentia were climbing out.

'That must be the mint!'

Both boys sprinted forward, with Balbus waddling after them, calling out to them to wait.

The three of them stepped through the door, and Perry let out a gasp.

This is where it's going to happen! he thought, and he looked around frantically for Valentia.

36

THE IMPERIAL MINT

THE BUILDING WAS FILLED WITH the deafening *clang-clang* of hammers on metal and in the room beside Perry, men used claw-like pincers to pour streams of boiling liquid in a haze of sparks and flames.

Valentia's clothes are going to catch on fire! realised Perry. *I need a heavy cloth to smother the flames . . .*

His hands flew to his woollen cloak and he struggled to unpin it, his fingers shaking.

'Carotus, Peregrinus,' called Valentia, appearing from another room.

Perry leapt towards her, still struggling with his cloak. She was holding out a shiny coin to show them.

'They're making them in here,' she shouted over the din, and stepped back through the door.

'Wait!' cried Perry, finally dragging off his cloak, and charging in behind her.

But there was no fire in this room. Three men were clustered around an anvil, working so fast, Perry could hardly see what they were doing. One of them pulled a small shiny circle from a basket and rested it on the anvil. The next slid a chunk of metal on top, and the third swung a mallet in the air.

CRASH.

As the mallet was lifted, the little disc, with a pattern now stamped on both sides, was dropped into a bag.

Then, without a break, they did it again. And again. They were so quick, the coins were clattering into the bag almost as fast as Perry could count.

On the far side of the room a small man with a tuft of white hair on top of his head was keeping tally. He bobbed like a bird, counting each coin as it dropped in the bag, and making marks on a wax tablet.

Maximus stood beside him, arms crossed, a small, satisfied smile on his lips.

'*Eia*, don't block the door,' yelled a voice, and a slave boy pushed past Perry with another basket of blank discs and dropped it on the floor. 'Any to go, Rissus?' he called.

Without taking his eyes from his counting, the small man jerked his head towards a full bag at his feet.

'Right,' said the boy, and, snatching it up with a clanking noise, he trotted out of the room.

Maximus strolled over to Perry and Carotus. 'Fetch Balbus,' he ordered. He turned to Valentia. 'Daughter, there are people I have to see now. Balbus and the boys will take you home.'

Perry and Carotus found the old man still peering through the door into the first room.

'See how they make the blanks,' he quavered. 'They heat the metal and pour it into the moulds . . .'

Valentia came skipping towards them, and as she drew close, Perry's grip tightened on his cloak. She smiled as she brushed past them into the room, sweeping out her arm towards the fiery, hot metal.

'Did you see . . .' she started to say, but Perry was throwing his cloak around her, dragging her back.

'Peregrinus, what are you doing?!' she exclaimed.

'Don't go so close, it's too dangerous,' he panted.

She laughed. 'It's too hot in here, anyway. Come on, let's look at the docks again. I couldn't see properly before. Father made me keep the curtain shut.'

Perry staggered out of the building with relief. But they still had to get through the perilous world of swinging cranes and overloaded carts, a crowded bridge and a deep river . . .

Balbus toddled along, oblivious, reeling off his quotes, and Carotus was useless. He still believed in his silly spell.

Perry heaved a sigh when they left the dock area behind.

Valentia, though, seemed in no hurry to get home.

'This is fun,' she said. 'We can go anywhere we want! Balbus won't notice.'

She meandered along, disappearing in and out of the crowds, and stopping at every shop they passed.

I need eyes in the back of my head, thought Perry. Every time he blinked, she had vanished, bobbing up a moment later with something to show them.

'Look at these,' she giggled, slipping her feet, shoes and all, inside a huge pair of clogs with sheepskin lining.

And, 'See this lamp,' she squawked, holding up a bronze lamp in the shape of a bare foot. 'It's even got toenails!'

Enticing smells wafted from the other side of the road, and Perry and Carotus hurried to follow Valentia as she crossed over to a take-away food shop.

Customers lined the footpath, shouting and pointing into big clay pots of food set into the countertop. The three children stretched on their toes, trying to see what the shopkeeper was dishing out. Behind her, more pots were simmering and steaming on the stove.

'Valentia,' puffed the old tutor, coming up to join them, 'this is not a suitable place for a respectable young lady to eat.'

Valentia tossed him a mischievous smile. 'I'm hungry,' she insisted.

At that moment, a gap opened up, and she and the boys pushed their way to the counter.

Perry peered at the warm, disgusting mixtures in the pots. How long had they been sitting here, breeding germs?

Valentia wrinkled her nose too, and pointed at some cheese. 'I'll have that,' she said.

'Are we going home now?' asked Perry hopefully.

'No, I want to look at more shops,' said Valentia.

Perry groaned.

It was late afternoon when they finally turned for home.

'Dinnertime, and we haven't had to work all day!' sang Carotus.

'Dinner,' sighed Perry with relief.

Valentia never went out after dinner. Once they were home, surely she'd be safe.

His feet were dragging now, barely able to move.

He'd had no idea how exhausting it would be, trying to keep an eye on Valentia for hours and hours.

At last he spotted the grand entrance to the town house, just a few doors ahead of them.

Nearly safe! he thought. *I've done it!*

'See, the magic worked,' hissed Carotus, sidling up beside him.

As Perry rolled his eyes, the door to the town house opened and the doorman peeked out. A kitten face appeared at his feet, and then a little ginger shape came bounding towards them.

'Bucco!' cried Valentia. She scooped him up and nuzzled her face against his fur. 'Did you miss me?' she asked, then she thrust him into Perry's arms. 'I'm tired,' she declared. 'You carry him.'

'*You're* tired?!' Perry exclaimed.

At that moment, out of the corner of his eye, he saw a wooden wheel come bowling down the road all by itself. At the same instant, he heard the horrible screeching sound of something grating along stone, and a man bellowing.

Perry flung round. A mule cart was lurching towards the footpath, dragging a broken axle, its load teetering and falling . . .

'Valentia!' he screamed.

He threw the kitten aside and hurled himself forward. He felt his hands connect with Valentia, and then he was slammed facedown on the ground, a huge weight piling on top of his legs.

For a second he lay stunned, then he managed to raise himself to look up. Valentia was standing in front of him, staring down, her face white.

'Peregrinus! Are you all right?'

'Young man, are you injured?' The mule cart driver leapt off his seat and crouched down by Perry's head. 'My whole load of sand has fallen on top of you,' he said in a worried voice.

'*Fortune favours the brave!*' intoned Balbus.

Carotus stood looking down with his hands on his hips and a smirk on his face.

I did it, thought Perry, *I really did it. I saved her!*

He started to laugh, a chuckle that started way down at his toes and worked its way up till it burst out of his mouth.

'I don't think I'm hurt,' he chortled. 'But . . .' He wiggled. 'I can't get up. I'm stuck!'

The cart driver, Carotus, Balbus, and even Valentia knelt down to scrape away the sand, and two ragged boys ran over to help. People began to crowd around.

'Is he injured?'

'What happened?'

'Do you need a drink, boy?'

Then, suddenly, everyone straightened up, and turned away from him.

'Who's that?'

'Must be an official from the emperor.'

'He's going very fast!'

Perry lifted his head.

They were all looking up the road, and he could hear the clatter of hoofs over their loud chatter. He twisted his head, trying to peer through the forest of legs.

A grand, horse-drawn carriage was speeding down the road. Perry glimpsed it swerve around a slow, plodding cart, and saw pedestrians leap out of its way. He felt the pounding of hoofs coming closer.

And now it was so close, he could see the jingling silver decorations swinging from its sides.

Then a woman shrieked, and a little boy burst into tears as she dragged him off the road. His half-eaten tart fell with a *splat* on the cobblestones.

The next instant, greedy little Bucco bounded off the footpath and darted towards it.

'No,' gasped Valentia, and she jumped off the footpath after him, right in the path of the thudding hoofs.

'Noooo!' screamed Perry.

In a last, desperate heave, he fought at the weight pinning him down. But he knew, in a horrifying flash, there was nothing he could do. The past could not be changed. Valentia was about to die, in front of his eyes.

And it was me who caused it! he thought, tears burning his throat. *Because I dropped her precious cat!*

Then something came flying over him, and Perry stared in amazement as Carotus soared over the pile of sand in one impossible leap and shot forward like a bullet from a gun.

For a moment, the world stood still.

There was no sound: only the sight of Valentia, in the middle of the road, bending over the little ball of orange fur. Perry could see the frantic face of the driver, he could see the hoofs of the horses rearing up, about to crush her . . . Then Carotus was on top of her, dragging her out of the way, and the carriage was thundering past, and the world was filled with sound again.

Everyone was screaming and shouting, and Perry was sobbing in relief.

And a small orange kitten crouched in the middle of the road, lapping up the contents of a tart.

37

HERO

PERRY LAY FACEDOWN, LISTENING TO the shouts of praise being heaped on Carotus.

'What a brave boy!'

'So lucky you saw!'

'As Cicero said, *A true friend can be seen in times of danger.*'

I didn't do a thing in the end, thought Perry angrily. *I just lay here, stuck. It was Carotus who did the saving.*

Pressing his face into his arms, he tried to smother the ache of jealousy and regret . . .

He heard Habita come out and shoo Valentia inside, and hands began to scrape at the pile of sand again.

A minute later, he wriggled free and stood up. But he kept his head bent, dusting off his tunic and leggings, till the last exclamations of praise, and the voices of the other people, had faded away.

Then he looked up.

Carotus was standing alone, his face shining with pride.

'Hello, big hero,' said Perry, trying not to sound jealous.

Carotus's expression changed.

'You're the real hero,' he muttered, and he gave Perry a rueful smile. 'I didn't even see the cat on the road. The sand was in the way. If you hadn't screamed . . .'

Perry stared at him. 'You mean . . .'

Carotus pulled a face. 'I don't think the spell would have worked,' he admitted. 'If you hadn't been here, if you hadn't screamed, Valentia would have been killed.'

Perry felt a flood of joy exploding inside him. *I did* do it. *I did* save her! he thought. *And now . . . And now I can go home!*

Beaming, he turned towards the house. Mule-face was standing in the doorway, glaring.

'Boys!' he bellowed.

'Time to get back to work,' said Carotus.

Perry was almost floating with excitement and happiness. He couldn't wipe the smile off his face as he helped to serve the dinner.

And it doesn't matter if I get into trouble. I'm going home anyway, he thought.

Pouring water into Valentia's wine, Perry remembered all the mistakes he'd made at the first dinner, and how strange everything had seemed.

Now it will feel strange sitting at a normal dining table again, eating with a knife and fork, he thought. *And I won't be drinking wine anymore for a while!*

The first dishes were mussels – Perry recognised the pointy black shells – and, 'What are those?' he whispered, sniffing at a dish of long green stalks.

'Thistles done in fennel and mint.'

Perry chuckled. He'd have to tell Dad to start cooking the weeds from their garden.

'So, Valentia, I hear you had a misadventure on your way home,' said Maximus, tipping his head back and slurping in a long thistle stalk.

'Yes, I nearly got killed,' said Valentia. 'By a horse carriage, but . . .'

'And how did that happen?'

'It was going too fast,' Valentia complained. 'Mules don't go that fast. But Carotus saved me. He pulled me out of the way. Isn't that brave, Father?'

Maximus glanced at Carotus. 'I am very pleased with you, boy.' He peered into the mussel pot and lifted out a shell, dripping with sauce.

'Father,' Valentia burst out, 'Carotus wants to be

an apprentice to . . . to that man who painted our walls. I wish . . .'

She gulped, and Perry stared at her in astonishment. Valentia had sworn she could never make a suggestion like this to her father.

'Father, I wish . . .' Valentia's voice trembled, but she went on. 'As a reward, could you let Carotus become his apprentice?'

Maximus snapped open the shell. It was the only sound in the room. Everyone else seemed to be holding their breath.

Then he began to chuckle, a deep, rumbling laugh. 'Why not?' he said.

He sucked the mussel from the shell, and glanced round for the bowl to wash his fingers.

Valentia turned to the boys with a proud smile on her face, and Carotus gazed back at her with wonder.

38

WILL IT WORK?

'YOU CAN'T GO YET. YOU'VE got to come to the circus with us!'

Dinner was over and Perry, Valentia and Carotus were whispering together outside the dining room.

'Everyone says it's really exciting,' hissed Carotus. 'Like that kick-ball you're always talking about. You've got to come!'

Perry pictured the circus in his head. He'd seen a model in the Arles museum. It wasn't just acrobats, he knew. It was chariot-racing – horses hurtling around a track, chariots bumping along behind them, slewing and crashing into each other, chariot-eers cracking their whips, crowds cheering . . .

For an instant, he wavered.

I've been living in Roman times for four months, he thought, *and I haven't seen a single gladiator fight or a chariot race.*

But . . . no, it was time to go home.

'When tomorrow comes, I'm leaving,' he said firmly.

As darkness fell, he dragged his sleeping mat to Valentia's door again. He would wait here till the end of the night, to be sure nothing happened.

Inside the room, he could hear the reassuring murmur of two voices – Habita's and Valentia's – but after a while, the talking stopped. Soon, there came the soft, rhythmic sound of Habita's snores.

Very slowly, Perry opened the door and peeked in. A lamp in the corridor behind him sent a glimmer of light shining into the room. On one side, he could see the large, humped form of the nursemaid, and on the other . . .

A slight figure lay on her bed, turned away from the door. All he could see was her dark plait and the gentle rise and fall of her shoulder. He stared for a long time, waiting for her to turn, but she lay still, deeply asleep.

'Goodnight, Valentia,' he whispered. 'Goodbye.'

Carefully, he closed the door again, lay down, and closed his eyes.

He was woken by a rattling noise. He jerked

upright, then recognised the sound. It was charcoal being spread on the kitchen stove.

It's morning! he thought. *Time to go home.*

Springing to his feet, he flew towards the slaves' room to fetch his old clothes and the stylus. The grey light of dawn was already seeping through the house, and people were beginning to stir. But the three blond boys lay snoring in a row. With a grin, Perry pretended to trip on Vibius as he passed.

'Wha ...?' Vibius sprang awake, bumping the next boy along, and a moment later all three of them were awake, grumbling and rubbing their eyes.

Carotus was waiting for Perry by the open clothes chest.

'Here,' he said, pulling out the yellow tunic Perry had been wearing when he'd first arrived at the villa.

Perry stared at it, remembering how he'd complained that it looked like a dress. Now, it just looked normal. Mum had been right. That's what Roman boys wore.

He glanced at the other slaves moving around the room.

'I'd better get changed downstairs,' he said.

Barefoot and bare-legged, he skimmed down the stairs with Carotus beside him. But when they reached the dining room, they came to a startled halt.

291

'What are the doors doing shut?' demanded Perry. 'They're always open.'

Carotus stared at them, then reached out and thrust one open. Valentia was crouched down on the far side of the room, looking at the painted tree. She jumped up and spun round as they came in.

'Valentia!' gasped Perry.

She was wearing a long, undyed tunic – *Must be her nightdress*, thought Perry – with a whole reindeer pelt hugged around her for warmth.

'Quick, come in and close the doors before anyone sees you,' she warned. Then she held out a hand. 'I couldn't miss out on saying goodbye,' she said.

Perry bounded to her across the room.

'Are you really leaving us now?' she whispered.

Perry nodded. 'My family ... I can't stay away any longer,' he answered. 'Anyway, you've got all your new friends now. You don't have time for us slaves.'

Suddenly, she leaned forward to kiss his cheek. Her lips were very soft, but she didn't smell like a modern girl. Her skin was scented with olive oil and the fur around her smelt musty and unwashed.

She straightened up, laughing through tears. 'You're not really a slave though, are you?' she said. 'Oh, and I have to say thank you. Carotus told me if you hadn't screamed, he would never have known to rescue me.'

Perry met Carotus's eyes and the secret they couldn't tell passed between them.

Then Carotus punched Perry in the arm. 'All this soppy goodbye stuff – your stylus probably won't work anyway! Come on, are you going to try?'

He held out Perry's boxer shorts. 'Show Valentia these!' he said, flapping them in the air.

'What are they?' gasped Valentia.

Embarrassed, Perry snatched them out of Carotus's hands and pulled them on. 'They're under-clothes we wear in the future,' he mumbled.

A moment later, he was dressed in his old outfit: the tunic, the rope sandals, and the bit of string Mum had tied around his waist all those months ago. He gripped the stylus in his hand and crouched down next to the wall. He was shivering with nerves and excitement. He'd been waiting weeks and weeks to go home to his family and friends, to his real life . . .

'Thank you,' said Carotus gruffly. 'If you'd never come here, I wouldn't have the chance to be an apprentice.'

But Perry hardly heard him. All he could think about now was going home.

He placed the tip of the stylus against the wall – just below the tree so it wouldn't spoil the painting – and wrote the first letter: V.

He tried to swallow, but the blood was pounding too hard in his throat.

He scratched the next letter: A.

Vale, he thought, *goodbye. Only two letters to go.*

In a few seconds he was going to see this same painting all faded and peeling, behind a pane of glass.

His hand shook as he wrote the L.

Then, *Vale – that's the beginning of Valentia's name!* he realised suddenly.

He turned to look at her one last time. Her dark eyes were fixed on him, deep and intent.

He glanced at Carotus.

His friend had a smirk on his face. 'Bet it doesn't work,' he said.

'Bet it does,' croaked Perry.

And he wrote the last letter.

E.

39

A REAL BALL!

PERRY WAS SWAYING THROUGH THE AIR. Arms were struggling to hold him up, half-dropping him, people laughing.

'He's heavy. You shouldn't feed him so much, Dad,' said a girl's familiar voice.

He felt himself dropped roughly onto a chair. His eyes sprang open and he struggled to shake off the feeling of coming out of a dream.

A face peered down into his. 'You're awake! Were you just faking?' demanded the same voice.

'M–Melissa?' he mumbled. He stared at her. Why was she still wearing her costume?

Another face loomed into view, an anxious face wearing round, rimless glasses. 'Mum?!'

Perry shot upright and threw his arms around her.

'Oof,' she laughed. 'Maybe getting drunk is not so bad if it makes you give me hugs like this.'

'*Drunk*?'

'Very drunk,' she nodded. 'I knew that wine-tasting was a bad idea.'

'But . . .' Perry started to protest. Then he thought of all that disgusting wine he'd been drinking at every meal since he'd been gone. He probably stank of it!

'We found you dead drunk and fast asleep in that ruin,' smirked Melissa. 'We had to lug you all the way through the vineyard to the car, and then you snored worse than Dad the whole trip back to Arles.'

Perry gaped at her, then slowly looked around. They were in the guest lounge at Hôtel d'Arles and he was sitting in the squeaky leather armchair. Mum and Melissa were still wearing their costumes. And Dad was still dressed in his shorts and T-shirt even though it should be the middle of winter.

'H . . . have we only just got back from the festival?' he stammered.

All those months he'd lived through in the past . . . had it only been a couple of hours in modern times?

'No, we've just been to the moon,' snorted his sister. 'Of course we've just got back.'

Just got back! Then I haven't missed all the footy. I haven't missed the Grand Final! thought Perry.

'And we're going out for dinner now,' said Mum.

'So hurry up and get changed,' demanded Melissa.

Dinner! Proper food! Proper clothes! A real bathroom!

Perry sprang off the chair.

'You okay to walk now?' That was Dad, putting an arm around his shoulders.

I think I could fly! thought Perry, looking eagerly towards the stairs.

He rushed into the bathroom, flushed the toilet three times, just for fun, and stood at the smooth, shiny basin, splashing the warm, running water, and slithering scented soap between his fingers.

'Are you ever getting out of there?' demanded Melissa, hammering on the door. 'Come on, I'm starving.'

Perry threw off his costume, snatched up his shorts and plunged his hand in the pocket. He let out a huge, happy sigh as his fingers closed around his mini high-bounce ball. He pulled it out and flicked it on the floor, scooping it up in his hand. A real ball that bounced!

He strutted out of the bathroom, beaming, feeling as if he'd just been born again.

And now, he thought, *I can tell them about my adventures.*

A bubble of excitement welled up inside him as he held out the stylus.

'What's that?' asked Mum.

'An old Roman stylus I found in the vineyard,' said Perry.

Melissa's eyes widened. 'Cool! Is it worth a lot?'

'If it's genuine,' said Mum, and she took it, rolling it around and peering at it.

This was it. This was his moment.

'I know it's genuine,' Perry began. 'I used it to scratch words in the ground, and . . .'

And then he stopped.

His family hadn't even missed him. They didn't even know he'd been anywhere. There was no way they were going to believe he'd gone back in time.

Perry felt like the bladder bursting on the rose bush. He'd been planning for weeks how he was going to describe everything for them, but now . . . They would all just laugh at him and say he'd been dreaming.

'It looks too new,' said Mum, handing back the stylus. 'It must be a reproduction.'

But as Perry stared at the thing in his hand, an awful thought swept over him. What if the whole adventure really had been a dream? Maybe he'd had heat stroke or something . . .

'Where do you all want to eat?' asked Mum.

At the foot of the stairs, the pane of glass on the painted wall winked as it caught the light. Perry dashed across to look at it. Yes, the painted tree was still there, and . . . His breath caught in his throat. He could see the orange and white stripes Carotus had painted. The kitten was there too. And . . . his heart was almost bursting out of his chest as he knelt down and peered below the tree. *Yes!* Two faint letters were still there, scratched into the paint: V . . . A . . .

He almost shouted out loud with excitement. It hadn't been a dream.

'Perry-y-y!'

He jumped to his feet again, grinning. It was fun hearing someone call him by his real name.

There were plenty of cafes nearby, but, somehow, they always ended up choosing the same one. They knew it had food they all liked.

'Your usual pizza, Perry?' asked Dad as the menus were placed in front of them.

At that moment, a waiter sidled past, holding a dish heaped with little shells.

Snails! thought Perry. He'd seen a lot of snails being eaten in the last four months but he'd never actually tasted any. 'Can I order snails?' he burst out.

He'd been waiting all this time to eat pizza again, but somehow, now that he could, it seemed a bit tame and ordinary.

There was a stunned silence around him.

Then, 'Good on you, mate,' said Dad. 'I'll join you.'

'You've got to be kidding!' groaned Melissa.

Perry looked at her. If he could taste roast dormice, he could manage a snail or two.

'We should try frogs' legs, too,' he declared. 'That's what you're supposed to eat in France.'

'I think we brought the wrong boy back with us,' gasped Mum.

The snails were served with special little forks, and Perry thought of the guests in the town house using the pointy handles of their spoons.

'You're not really eating them, are you?' asked Melissa, watching in horror.

Perry smiled smugly as he scooped out the rubbery bits of flesh coated in garlic butter. He was almost disappointed there were no strange flavours mixed in, like honey or rotten fish.

'So,' said Mum, 'we're off to Constantine's Bathhouse tomorrow morning.'

Perry nearly burst out laughing. He'd washed in that bathhouse nearly every afternoon for months. That was one place he didn't need to visit. But there was somewhere else he desperately wanted to go.

'Let's do the museum again, too,' he said. He had to make sure Valentia's coffin was gone.

'Fine with me,' said Mum.

'No way!' protested Melissa. 'It was boring enough the first time.'

'You wait in the car, then,' said Perry. 'But I need to look at something.'

Melissa stared at him. 'Please don't tell me you're going to look at the dead people again,' she said.

Before Perry could think of an answer, Dad yawned and stretched. 'I'm for bed,' he groaned. 'Come on. It's been a long day.'

40

ARLES MUSEUM

PERRY WOKE AT DAWN. He was used to early morning starts now. He closed his eyes and tried to keep his head on the pillow.

You've been longing for this soft bed for months, he scolded himself. *Stay here!*

But the next instant, his bare feet were touching the carpet and he was tiptoeing across the floor to Melissa's bed.

'Wake up,' he whispered, 'let's go for a walk.'

She opened an eye and glowered at him. 'Are you mad? It's not even morning yet.'

'Come on,' he pleaded. 'It'll be fun. There might be a bakery open,' he added temptingly.

But Melissa's eyes were firmly closed again.

Sighing, Perry straightened up. He'd been hoping

to find a hot, crunchy pie like Valentia had eaten every morning on the way to school.

Then all at once he realised he didn't need Melissa. He could go out on his own ...

Quietly, he found some clothes to put on. A room key lay on the little desk, and Perry scooped it up, along with a few coins from Dad's pocket.

He won't mind if I take them to buy breakfast, Perry decided.

He pulled the door behind him and listened a moment. There was no stirring from inside. Flying down the stairs, he felt light-headed with freedom.

Outside, the narrow lane was almost empty. He swung along the footpath, peering at the dilapidated three-storey buildings crowding in on both sides. There was no sign of the wide, bustling street of Roman times. There were no children playing knucklebones, no hens clucking in cages, no customers haggling noisily with shopkeepers at open storefronts ...

But there was a patisserie! He stared at the macarons, eclairs, glazed strawberry tartlets, chocolate cake – chocolate! He hadn't tasted chocolate for months.

And then his gaze fell on a fig tart. He'd thought he'd never want to see a fig again, but now that was the one thing he wanted most in the world.

He paid for it and wandered back slowly along the road, relishing every bite.

When he opened the door of the hotel room, Mum sprang up, startled, in bed.

'Where've you been?' she cried.

'Just for a walk.'

'In the street ... on your own?' She sounded horrified. 'You could have got lost!'

Perry wanted to laugh. *Mum, I've survived on my own for four months in a strange world,* he thought. *I'm not a little kid anymore.*

'What time does the bathhouse open?' he asked, licking the last trace of fig off his fingers.

'Nine, I think,' yawned Mum.

'*Eia*, everyone, get up then,' he cried.

Melissa crawled out of bed, groaning. 'Mum, you're right. I think we did bring the wrong boy home with us!'

Perry hustled them all through breakfast, but at last they were in the hire car, heading for the bathhouse.

He peered out the window, suddenly excited to see it again. At least there was one thing left from his world of the past. It was only when he caught sight of the familiar curved, stripy wall that he realised, with dismay, that most of the huge, grand building was missing. The courtyard where he'd played ball, the changing room, the cold baths – were all gone.

At the entrance gate, he discovered that even the floors had fallen away. They had to walk down wooden ramps and steps to get into the ruins.

Mum immediately darted from side to side, spouting tidbits.

'This is the *hypocaust* – the heating system,' she cried, waving her arms. 'It's amazing. We're standing right inside it. Look, you can see how it worked. See that arch? They burnt wood in there and the heat flowed under the floor and up the walls.' She rushed forward to look up at the big vaulted room at the end. 'This was the *caldarium* – the room with the hot baths . . .'

Perry remembered the steam billowing from the hot water, the heat radiating up from the floor . . .

'They had to wear funny wooden shoes to protect their feet,' he said.

Mum spun round. 'What? How do you know?'

'Uh . . .' He'd spoken without thinking. 'It . . . it was in that book you gave us.'

'Oh, that's something I didn't know! That book had good information.'

Perry smiled to himself. *If only you knew!*

'Now, look,' Mum went on, 'this is where one of the baths used to be. We are standing right inside it.'

Perry looked at the rubble around them. Was that the seat where he used to sit with Carotus?

A lump suddenly rose in his throat. All the time he'd been stuck in the past he'd been wanting his family and friends, but now ... he was missing Carotus and Valentia! He pictured that last moment, kneeling on the floor, the stylus in his fingers, looking back at them ...

The stylus!

He felt for it, nestled in his pocket. What if ...

'Important men used the baths as a place to socialise,' said Mum.

'The slaves did too!' said Perry. 'Er, that was in the book too,' he added.

As Mum rattled off another tidbit, Perry felt Melissa sidle up next to him. 'It did not say that in the book,' she whispered. 'And there was nothing about wooden shoes either. You're making it up.'

He blinked at her. He didn't know Melissa had even opened the book. So, she wasn't as uninterested in all the Roman stuff as she pretended to be.

'I must have read it in one of the tourist leaflets then,' he muttered.

He began to wonder if maybe he could tell Melissa about his adventure one day. Of course she would say she didn't believe him, but ... it would be fun to share it anyway.

All he wanted to do now, though, was get to the museum. For once, he was just as impatient as Melissa and Dad to finish looking at a ruin.

'Off to the museum!' he said, when they finally piled back in the car.

By the time they pulled up outside the bright, shiny-blue building, though, his stomach was churning with nerves. What if the coffin was still there?

'You've got ten minutes!' Melissa warned. 'Come on, Dad, we're getting ice creams.'

As the two of them headed off, Perry almost followed. He could pretend he'd just wanted to play the games again. They were set up in the garden near the food van . . .

But he forced himself to follow Mum inside.

'I'm so glad you like museums,' gushed Mum. 'Go wherever you like. I want to look at those mosaics again.'

The museum was built in a huge triangle around a courtyard. He'd have to go all the way around to get to where the coffin was.

Where it used to be, he corrected himself.

He glanced in a glass case as he set off, then jerked to a halt. Lying in front was a lamp – a lamp with a tiger on it – just like the one Valentia had given him and Carotus for New Year.

He bent down to read the label. Under a lengthy explanation in French were the words:

These household objects, dating from the early fourth century CE, were all uncovered during renovation work at Hôtel d'Arles.

Perry felt a shiver of shock. He raised his eyes and scanned the other things inside. There was a bone backscratcher with a tiny hand on the end, a green wineglass, a whole lot of cracked clay pots . . . and a set of knucklebones.

Mum came up behind him and looked over his shoulder.

'Things like this make the past come to life, don't they?' she said. 'You can picture real, ordinary people using them.'

'Yes, real people,' he whispered.

He was desperate now to make sure the coffin was gone. He sped off, moving as fast as he could without actually running.

There were coffins dotted everywhere: big stone boxes with elaborate decorations, and the names of the dead carved on the side. But the main collection was further on.

He was nearly there . . .

And now he was among them, dodging frantically past carvings of faces and figures in togas. Valentia's had been right near the end . . .

And then he stopped, feeling as if all the blood was draining out of his body. It was still there. It hadn't disappeared. It was just where it had been before.

'It can't be,' he whispered. 'What went wrong?'

Slowly, very slowly, he dragged his feet forward and stared at the name, Camilla Valentia, carved into the stone. The inscription seemed longer than he remembered. He dropped his gaze to the translation below.

To Camilla Valentia

Dearest and most loved

Dedicated by her husband Ausonius Leontius Rufus . . .

'Rufus?! Her *husband*?!'

Perry's eyes flew to the last words.

She lived 55 years.

Fifty-five years!

Perry almost shouted, and punched his hands in the air. He had done it! He had changed the past. Fifty-five was a long life for someone from Roman times.

But what about Carotus? What happened to him? Did he get his freedom the way that painter said he might?

As Perry ran back to the others, he slid his hand in his pocket and closed his fist around the precious stylus.

Maybe, one day . . . he thought.

GLOSSARY

Amphitheatre – Stadium for shows such as gladiator fights.

Amphora (amphorae) – Large clay pot(s) used to transport wine/oil.

Archaeologist – Expert who investigates the past from physical remains.

Barbarians – Roman word for people outside Roman Empire.

Château – Grand country house in France.

Ecce – 'Look!' in Latin.

Eia – 'Hey!' in Latin.

Forum – Public square in centre of Roman city.

Forum Julii – Roman name for town of Fréjus, in France.

Garland – Decorative chain of flowers and leaves.

Gaul – Roman region mostly equivalent to modern France.

Gladiators – Men trained to fight to entertain the public.

Ides of November/January – Thirteenth day.

Latin – Language spoken by Romans and used in their empire.

Legionary – Roman soldier.

Mantle – Shawl-like cloth draped around the body.

Milestone – Stone showing distance in miles to a big city. A Roman mile was 1.5 km.

Must – Juice from grape-treading.

Papyrus – Writing material made from a plant.

Parchment – Writing material made from thin leather.

Press – Device to press juice or oil from fruit or olives.

Roman – Person living anywhere in the Roman Empire or their way of life.

Spindle – Tool used in making woollen thread.

Strigil – Curved metal stick to scrape oil and sweat off skin.

Stylus – Shaped stick for writing in wax.

Terracotta – Baked clay, often reddish coloured.

Toga – Large woollen mantle traditionally worn by Romans.

Une journée romaine – A Roman Day (French).

Vah – Latin exclamation of surprise, anger or joy.

Via – Road (Latin).

Vineyard – Place where grapes are grown on vines.

Winch – Rope wound around rod, used to lift heavy object.

Wreath – Circle of flowers or leaves worn on the head.

AUTHOR'S NOTE

I GREW UP IN A house without television. My sisters and I used to spend a lot of time making up stories, drawing pictures and cutting out paper dolls together. When I was ten, I started writing a novel set in ancient Roman times. I only got as far as the first page but the opening scene – a boy, dressed in a tunic, running down a cobbled street – flickered in and out of my mind for the next fifty years . . .

When the three of us grew up, I became an author and illustrator, Miriam became a teacher of French and Japanese, and Tamara went on to become an archaeologist, specialising in the Roman Empire.

One day, I jokingly suggested to Tamara that we collaborate on a book together. She jumped at the idea, bubbling with excitement.

'What would we write about?' she asked.

'Ancient Rome, of course!' I said, my mind flying to that image of the boy running down a cobbled street.

It was fun immersing ourselves in Roman times – we even went grape-treading together – but after two years, I didn't have a plot. Maybe that boy was never going to find his story!

And then, the breakthrough came.

'When a Roman child died,' Tamara told me, 'the parents wrote the exact number of years, months and days their child had lived on the coffin.'

That was it! I'd found the key to my plot.

And so, after fifty years, the boy became Perry, I finished his story, and Tamara made sure ... but no, I'll let her tell you for herself. Let's just say that I strongly suspect the character of Perry's mum is based on Tamara ...

Anna Ciddor, Melbourne, 2021

RESEARCHER'S NOTE

AFTER STUDYING AND TEACHING ROMAN archaeology and history for many years, I was thrilled when Anna suggested we collaborate on a story set in ancient Roman times. This was my chance to see the scraps of ancient things I had studied for years come to life! We decided to set the story in southern Gaul (now France) in the early 4th century, my favourite period of history, and we chose the exact years 313–314 CE.

However, almost at once, Anna started asking me difficult questions. 'What did slaves eat for breakfast?' 'What rude names would they call each other?' 'How did children celebrate birthdays?' 'How did people tell the time?'

To answer her, I had to read more than a thousand books and articles (including some written in Latin), contact archaeologists and historians around the world, and try to decipher tiny details from old Roman paintings and mosaics!

I was determined to make sure all the details Anna wanted about life in 4th-century Gaul were correct – or, as Perry's mum would say, 'authentic!'

The Truth behind the Book

The villa

Villa Rubia is modelled on a real Roman villa uncovered by archaeologists at a place called Taradeau in southern France. It is now just a ruin, as described in the story, but archaeologists worked out that these were the remains of a mansion, a courtyard with columns, a large, red-painted pond, and presses for wine and oil.

The town house

Maximus's town house is modelled on a real Roman town house excavated in Arles. Archaeologists found wall-paintings, mosaic floors and a marble pool there, as well as a small folding knife like the one Carotus has in the story!

Eating

The descriptions of food and meals all come from Roman poems, letters, and recipes. Dinner party hospitality included slaves washing guests' hands – and feet! – and archaeologists have discovered fishponds in very rich villa dining rooms. Roman writers mention garlands strewn over dining couches and fried fish wrapped in papyrus. Researchers think Roman carrots were probably pale yellow – and you can still occasionally find old-style yellow carrots in shops or restaurants.

Special note: what Perry calls 'mice' are really European dormice (small animals a bit like squirrels) and the fish sauce, garum, was not mouldy, as Perry thinks, but fermented (like yoghurt, wine or soy sauce).

Wine and oil presses

To make wine and oil, the Romans squeezed grapes and olives using presses. For the earlier type of press, the winch press, a lot of effort was needed to drag down the pressing beam with ropes. Screw presses were easier because the huge screw did the work if the men just turned it by walking in a circle.

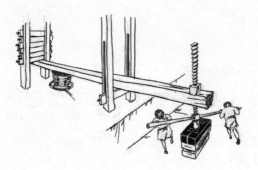

Slavery

There were many different ranks and types of slaves in the Roman Empire: beautifully dressed slaves to serve the master or mistress, young handsome slaves with long hair for dinner parties, secretaries, tutors, hairdressers, doormen, musicians, and slaves to work in the kitchen or on the farm. Many people had slaves, not just the very rich. There were also many other sorts of workers, like the hired men who come for the grape harvest in the story. Poor free people found life very hard, because there was very little government help compared to today.

Roman slaves were often freed by their masters as a reward or mark of affection. They would then become normal citizens, and might be set up in business by their former masters, so they could become very rich and successful.

Rich children were cared for by slaves like Valentia's nursemaid Habita, rather than by their parents.

Château Taradel
The winery in the story is modelled on a real winery called Château de Saint Martin located near the villa ruins. That winery really does have a basement cellar, a historical display and an open day in September.

The stylus
When archaeologists excavated the villa at Taradeau, they found grape-cutting knives, coins, and fragments of green glass. We imagined that Perry could find

something in the vineyard nearby as farmers in Europe often turn up Roman objects when they are digging the ground.

Note: If you visit an archaeological or historical site, you must *never* try to dig or take anything away, like Perry does. Only characters in stories are allowed to do that! Ancient remains belong to everyone, and every find needs to be studied and looked after in a museum where everyone can enjoy it.

The painted tree

Many buildings in Europe really do contain bits of walls from Roman times. On rare occasions, remains of wall paintings have been found, sometimes showing scenes of the owner's country villa, a garden, or animals. Although Hôtel d'Arles is fictional, it is inspired by typical hotels in Arles, and it could have a Roman painting, discovered during renovations, installed as a feature in the lounge.

Strange but true

When archaeologists discovered the weight stone from the oil press at the villa of Taradeau, it really did have a hole drilled in the wrong place! This must have happened when the owners changed to using a screw instead of a winch in their press – just like in the story.

At Saturnalia, slaves and masters really did swap places.

Valentia's white birthday outfit is 'whiffy' because the Romans used sulphur (which smells like rotten eggs) to bleach clothes.

Did you notice in the story that Emperor Constantine's court was in Augusta Treverorum (modern Trier)? That's because at this time, the Roman emperors no longer lived in Rome! They moved around to different important cities.

Want to know more?

To find out more details, or learn some of the secrets of my detective work, visit https://annaciddor.com/tamaras-secrets/

I extend a huge 'thank you' to the many people named in the acknowledgements who helped with my research. Any errors are my own.

Tamara Lewit (School of Historical and Philosophical Studies, the University of Melbourne)

ACKNOWLEDGEMENTS

HEARTFELT THANKS TO ALL THE people who helped in the making of this book:

our sister Miriam, for her endless translations from French of emails and publications using difficult archaeological terms, and for her unstinting enthusiasm about the book;

Tamara's son Lucas Lewit-Mendes, for inspiration and his frequent advice on Latin;

all the Roman historians and archaeologists from around the world who generously shared their knowledge and invaluable advice, particularly Jacques Bérato, Paul Burton, Alexandra Chavarría, Arnaud Coutelas, Ash Green, Mary Harlow, Stéphane Martin, Tim Parkin, Yolanda Peña Cervantes, Eric Poehler, Richard Reece;

Alexandra Moreau from Château de Saint Martin;

the team at Allen and Unwin for the untiring dedication and attention to detail they have poured into publishing this book;

all the students, teacher-librarians and teachers at various schools who contributed opinions and suggestions.

ABOUT THE AUTHOR

ANNA CIDDOR HAS ALWAYS BEEN fascinated by the past. It would be her dream come true to really step through time! Instead, she immerses herself in research and hunts out the tiniest details so she can bring the past to life in her imagination – and in her books.

Anna's meticulous work has been recognised by a grant from the Literature Board of the Australia Council, three of her novels have been selected as Notable Books by the Children's Book Council of Australia, and several have been translated into other languages to be enjoyed around the world.

ABOUT THE RESEARCHER

WHEN TAMARA LEWIT WAS FIVE years old, she was one of those kids who could recite the name and characteristics of every dinosaur, but she was also, more unusually, obsessed by the ancient ruins and statues in a picture book on archaeology. Eventually, she gained a doctorate at the Institute of Archaeology in London.

She is now an Honorary Fellow in the School of Historical and Philosophical Studies at the University of Melbourne, and a Fellow of the Society of Antiquaries, London.

Her favourite research topics are wine and oil production and the later Roman Empire.

Also by Anna Ciddor . . .

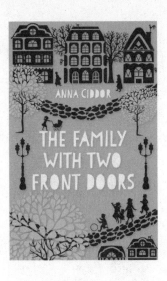

'A rare gem.'
Readers for Life

'A reminder of the beauty of simple lives,
and more profoundly the importance of
valuing individuals and families.'
Where the Books Are

'Ciddor's lively novel transports readers to
the Jewish quarter of the town of 1920s Lublin,
Poland ... and flows with energetic family
dynamics and warmth.'
Publishers Weekly

'Sophisticated, multi-layered and utterly
engaging ... a fascinating insight into the
lives of Orthodox Jews in the 1920s.'
Children's Books Daily

'Rich with historical detail . . . a fascinating window into everyday life in the 1960s.'
Sunday Telegraph

'A warm and funny family story.'
National Geographic Kids

'Ciddor paints a vivid picture . . . fans of historical fiction and diverse stories are sure to appreciate this tale.'
Books & Publishing

'[Ciddor] has drawn from her own family stories to give authenticity . . . a warm, charming story.'
Good Reading